THE EDGE OF HOPE

WRAK-AYYA: THE AGE OF SHADOWS BOOK
ELEVEN

LEIGH ROBERTS

CONTENTS

Editing by Joy Sephton http://www.justemagine.biz
Cover design by Cherie Fox http://www.cheriefox.com

Sexual activities or events in this book are intended for adults.

ISBN: 978-1-951528-11-9 (ebook)
ISBN: 978-1-951528-18-8 (paperback)

Dedication

*To those of you who have stayed the course so far, and
who will continue on the journey with me, to answering
the question—*

What If?

CHAPTER 1

The cold air bit into Pajackok's face as he steered his horse, Atori, in the direction of the shelter he had built after leaving the Brothers' village for the first time. He looked back at Snana, who was riding Nawaba, making sure she was not having any trouble keeping up. She smiled that she was fine.

When they finally arrived, it was already nightfall. Pajackok pulled the supply bags from his horse and set them down before helping Snana with hers. They had brought warmer tunics, leggings, and foot coverings for their return to the village in a few weeks, by when the cold weather would have taken hold.

Pajackok quickly had a fire going outside the shelter, and they sat in front of it enjoying the warmth, made drowsy by the crackling of the flames and the smell of the charred wood. Tired from their travels, they soon went inside and quickly fell asleep.

The next morning, Snana rolled over to find Pajackok watching her. "How long have you been awake?"

"Not long. We were both too tired even to consummate our bonding!"

"I think I fell asleep the minute we lay down. I am sorry!" said Snana.

He leaned down and kissed the top of her head, enjoying the feel of her soft hair brushing his nose. "I am going to start a fire outside. Come when you are ready. The temperature has already dropped again."

Pajackok exited the shelter and then stopped short. He surveyed the camp, and only now in the light of day did he realize that someone had been there while they were away at the village.

He quickly walked around, noticing that baskets had been moved and some of the firewood from the stack had been used. Luckily, the food stores he and Snana had gathered were barely touched. But, clearly, someone had been in their camp.

Just then, Snana came up behind him, a woven blanket wrapped around her shoulders.

"Someone was here," she said. "My medicine stores have been gone through, though it looks as if nothing was removed."

"Please stay close to the shelter today," Pajackok replied. "I am going to look for tracks."

Snana sat down by the fire to warm herself while her life-walker left to look around the area.

He returned after a short while. "There are horse tracks. And they are Waschini."

"At least they did not destroy anything. Perhaps they just needed a place to stay on their travels?" Snana said, trying to keep her voice lighthearted.

Pajackok nodded, though his forehead was still creased in a frown. "They are not fresh. But still, stay close to home; I will take care of anything that needs doing. At least for a few days, please."

Snana nodded and went back to huddling around the fire. She let out a long sigh and reached her feet out from under the blanket so they would warm faster. *Our homecoming is marred by these intruders; I pray they do not return.*

🦅

Several days passed without incident, then one morning, Pajackok left the shelter only to find fresh footprints around the camp. He went back in to throw on a tunic and grab a hatchet before going out to follow them. The tracks led up to a nearby ridge where there was evidence that several horses had been tied up. Pajackok frowned, angry with himself. A stranger had been walking around their camp sometime in the middle of the night. Surely the ponies must have nickered, yet he had not woken.

He returned to check on Snana, who was just waking up. She stretched and reached out for him.

"I am going to take Atori for a ride, and I will be back shortly; please stay inside."

Snana sat up. "What is wrong?"

"Waschini footprints in the dusting of snow this morning. I followed them to where they left on horseback."

Snana wrapped her blanket more closely around her. "May I come with you?"

"Hurry," he said and waited for her to throw on some warmer wraps and thicker foot coverings.

The two mounted up and followed the tracks up to the ridge. They followed the trail for a short distance, then, confident the Waschini were no longer in the area, returned home.

"We need to leave," Pajackok proclaimed as he dismounted. "It is no longer safe here."

"I do not want to leave," she said, eyes downcast. "Not yet. It looks as if they have left. If they wanted to hurt us, they would have done so last night while we were sleeping."

Pajackok let out a long breath. "It is not safe, Snana. We are leaving in the morning."

Snana secured Nawaba, turned on her heels, and walked off. She busied herself the rest of the day with trying to think of a way to change his mind. She wanted some time for themselves before returning to the village with all its distractions.

The next morning, as Snana was starting the fire, she heard a horse snort and turned to see three Waschini men watching her from the ridge she and Pajackok had inspected the day before. One of the horses pawed the ground in impatience, perhaps objecting to the cold.

Snana did not move, but her eyes darted around the perimeter of the camp; Pajackok could not be far away. She knew the Waschini had seen her, and so she rose to her feet. Using what she remembered of the Whitespeak her mother had taught her, and hoping Pajackok would hear, she called out. "Welcome. Are you in need of food? Or warmth?" She glanced down at the fire and swept her hand toward it before looking back up at them.

Two of the three Waschini grinned and exchanged glances. A chill crawled up Snana's spine.

One of the men snapped his reins, and they all started down the slight rise of the ridge, horses carefully picking their way down the incline. She kept her eyes pinned on them and felt a small trickle of relief when she heard rustling in the undergrowth and knew it had to be Pajackok returning.

The three men looked close in age and were wearing typical Waschini clothing with hats and leather boots. They all seemed scruffy—as if they had been on the road for some time.

The first man muttered something to the second

and pointed to where Pajackok had just emerged from the brush.

Pajackok thrust his stack of branches to the ground, where they scattered next to him. He dusted off his hands, felt for the hatchet at his waistband, and strolled over to Snana as he addressed the men. "Why are you here? What do you want?" he called out, on the off-chance they might understand him.

Snana stood frozen as she listened to their next words.

"Too bad he showed up. Looks like he's going to spoil our fun," said the first man.

"Oh, I don't think one local is going to stop the three of us," the second grinned.

The third man spoke up, "Stop it. Stop talking like that. We're going to continue on our way and leave them be."

"Who put you in charge?" frowned the first.

"They're not bothering anyone, and we aren't going to bother them. It was wrong enough that we entered their camp last night. I should never have allowed it."

"Look at all this land," said the second man, gesturing. "What use is it to them? All they do on it is hunt. It could be worth a fortune."

"As long as Pa isn't with us, I'm in charge, and you'd best remember it," the third man said. "Now, let's move on." He turned his horse and started away from the camp. "No doubt Ma is worrying why we're taking so long to get home."

them. This time, there were no concerned stares or worried expressions, and they rode right into the middle of the village where Chief Is'Taqa soon arrived to greet them.

"We did not expect you back so soon," he said. "But I am glad you have returned home. Are you staying now?"

Snana dismounted and went to greet her father. "Yes, now we are back for good."

"Your mother and siblings will be pleased," the Chief replied.

Snana looked at Pajackok, waiting for him to tell her father what had happened. Then she realized that such a conversation should be held in private. "I will go and find Momma and let you talk," she said, calling out to the children as she left. They happily skipped along behind her.

"There was some trouble," Pajackok said, very gravely. The Chief nodded and motioned for the brave to follow him.

Once they were alone in Is'Taqa's shelter, Pajackok turned to the Chief, "There were Waschini men at our camp. They had entered it and left again before we arrived. Then they returned and prowled around outside while we were sleeping."

Chief Is'Taqa frowned. "Is there more?"

"Yes." And Pajackok described the confrontation and their subsequent decision to leave early.

"A wise move. Thank you for protecting my

daughter; I believe Snana has chosen well," Is'Taqa said, looking Pajackok squarely in the eye.

"Snana could make out their Whitespeak. She said they mentioned taking our land from us."

The Chief sighed deeply. "Come, let us get you both something to eat." He motioned for one of the braves to tend to the ponies. "You can share our shelter tonight. Tomorrow we will discuss whether you would like your own shelter, such as Oh'Dar and Acise have."

The two men walked off in silence.

CHAPTER 2

Oh'Dar had a lot of thinking time available as he and his grandparents made their way toward the Brothers' village. The farther away from Shadow Ridge they traveled, the more he relaxed. He could hear his grandmother and Ben chatting to each other on their horses as they traveled side by side behind him. Occasionally he looked back to see if they needed a break.

Though the weather was cooler, the trip had been uneventful. Ben took advantage of their time together to teach Oh'Dar more about navigating with the businessmen he was likely to encounter, such as bankers and storekeepers. He and Miss Vivian also told Oh'Dar more about Shadow Ridge's history, how the land had been fairly acquired by Oh'Dar's grandfather, though that was not always the case. Much was simply claimed through homesteading without regard for the locals' right to the land they'd always depended on.

As the travelers passed the smaller towns between Shadow Ridge and their destination, they stopped and camped for the night. Oh'Dar would ride into the town to pick up what provisions he could find. No one paid him much notice, no more than any other stranger, and all were very hospitable once they learned he had money to spend. He made sure to keep on good terms with everyone he met, not wanting to raise suspicion. He'd planned this as carefully as he could, needing to ensure there were no foul-ups.

He returned from his latest trip into a little town later than he intended. When he arrived, he found Ben and his grandmother sitting comfortably in front of a crackling fire. They looked up at the sound of Beauty's approaching hoofbeats.

Oh'Dar dismounted and took a while to tend to the horse. When that was done, he grabbed the saddlebags and walked over to Ben and Miss Vivian.

"Here you go," he said as he reached into the satchel and retrieved a parcel for his grandmother.

"Oh, what have we here?" Her eyes lit up.

She undid the knot that secured the rough packaging and opened it, angling it toward the firelight so she could see what was inside. "Oh," she said as she made out a collection of sweets, nuts, and dried jerky.

She handed out the jerky between them and tightly rewrapped the paper sack.

"I wish I could have brought you a home-cooked meal," Oh'Dar said.

"Thank you, but we're fine. I could certainly stand to lose a little weight, Grayson," she smiled.

The biscuits from Mrs. Thomas had disappeared days before, but it didn't matter; they were in good spirits over their new adventure.

Ben looked up at the twinkling stars overhead. "No cloud cover; we're going to lose heat from the land overnight."

"I'll pick up some more blankets in the next town," Oh'Dar said. "I'm not tired; I'll be glad to stay up and tend the fire for a while yet. Why don't you two try to get some sleep."

Ben turned to his wife, "Do you want to sleep in the wagon tonight, or here by the fire?"

Miss Vivian said, "Let's try here; the fire is so comforting. If we get cold, we can move inside."

Ben nodded, "Wake me when you get sleepy, son; I can take over from there."

After placing blankets on all the horses, Ben unpacked their own and spread them out over a dry spot not too far from the fire, trying to pick a place that naturally provided some cushioning. Once he had them arranged, he reached his hand out to help Miss Vivian up from the log she was sitting on.

She made a little oopf sound as he helped her to her feet. After brushing off the back of her skirt, she picked her way over to the sleeping places Ben had prepared.

Once Miss Vivian was comfortable, Ben covered her up and moved close to help keep her warm. She reached back to pat him and said good night. In the distance, coyotes started their evening calls. Oh'Dar sat for a long time tending to the fire, mesmerized by the dancing flames against the dark night. The familiar smell of the burning wood reminded him of the family night fires at the Brothers' Village. His thoughts drifted ahead to seeing his life-walker again and how happy he and Acise would be. He tried to imagine how his grandparents would feel stopping over at the village—if they'd feel as out of place as he had when he first came into the Waschini world. Though he was confident the Brothers would be kind to them, he knew it would still be a huge adjustment. *I hope I haven't made a mistake. I hope I haven't gotten them into something that will ultimately prove to be too much for them.*

While he was sitting there, his eye caught the tail of a shooting star as it streaked overhead. He let out a little gasp. *Mother would say that was a message of reassurance. So, I'll take it like that and try to stop worrying.*

The next morning, they packed, loaded up, and continued their travels. Oh'Dar took turns riding Beauty so his grandmother could sit on the wagon bench with Ben. Though she was an expert rider, long days in one position being jostled around on a horse was wearing on anyone.

At the next little town, Oh'Dar took the wagon with him. He did as he'd said and returned with a massive load of very nicely woven wool blankets.

"Gracious," Miss Vivian exclaimed. "Did you buy out the whole town?"

Oh'Dar laughed, "It looks like it, doesn't it? I just thought I should buy all I could find."

He set the blankets down and went back to the wagon. He had another surprise for them. Pillows.

"Where in the world did you get these?" she asked.

"For a small town, not even the size of the Webbs', they had a very well-stocked general store. And a large tavern. I also got you this." He tossed a fairly large flask to Ben.

Ben opened it and sniffed, "Cider?"

"Yes," said Oh'Dar. "It's apple pressing time!"

Ben handed it to his wife, who took a sip, smiled, and handed it back. "That is a treat!" she exclaimed.

"And this." He returned to Beauty, reached into the saddlebag, and retrieved an even larger package. He handed it to his grandmother, who opened it to find bread and cheese.

"Thank you, Grayson, this is much appreciated." She tore off a piece and put it to her nose, enjoying the yeasty smell before handing the rest to Ben.

Oh'Dar nodded, but he was still concerned about how they truly were faring.

"I think we should stay here today," he said. "This is a nice setting. The weather looks a little dark in the direction we're heading, and there are a couple of streams we have to cross before we get to the Webbs' village. I'd feel better if you were well-rested before we move on."

Ben got up to gather more branches and logs for the fire, and Oh'Dar headed into the brush in search of whatever berries he could find. It was late in the season, but the last crop of raspberries should still be out—if the birds hadn't finished them off.

When Oh'Dar returned with his pickings, he stopped to watch his grandparents sitting at the fire talking and laughing. *They seem happy; they really do. I need to control my worrying and enjoy the journey more. There isn't much road to cover before we pass by where the Webbs live.*

Oh'Dar divided up the berries, which they devoured.

"I could take my rifle and find us a turkey," Ben offered, "or a rabbit."

After thinking for a moment, Oh'Dar said, "Why don't we wait until we get a little farther away. I've always let it be assumed I was traveling alone because I don't want to cause any curiosity. I think we're far enough away that you wouldn't be recognized, but I'd still prefer that any stories about a stranger passing through are that he traveled alone."

Ben nodded and went back to tending the fire.

They need a really good meal, thought Oh'Dar. *I guess I'm just going to worry every bit of the way after all, and I have to resign myself to it. I wish I had my mother's faith.* That evening when they turned in, he was only able to stay awake a short while. He was exhausting himself, not only with worry but also from tiredness—staying up too late every night watching the fire lest his grandparents get cold as they slept outside.

The next morning, they arose early, all feeling the chill. Realizing he'd let the fire go out, Oh'Dar jumped to his feet and immediately went about rebuilding it.

Ben put his arms around Miss Vivian, trying to warm her up. Oh'Dar stopped what he was doing to bring his blanket over and added it to those already wrapped around her. She clasped it and pulled it more tightly to herself.

After they'd eaten breakfast, it was time to pack up and move on.

The day's journey was uneventful—mostly flat terrain covered with sparse brush, through which the horses had no trouble pulling the wagon. It was terrain that Oh'Dar had traveled several times, and he was saddened by the thought that this was almost certainly his last time. They interspersed long stretches of the journey with rest stops and periods of hunting. Oh'Dar gave Ben lessons on using a bow and arrow to avoid the noise a gun would make.

Ben drove the wagon, and Oh'Dar rode on Rebel. That day, Miss Vivian sat in the wagon, where she could rest and more easily keep warm.

As they traveled, Oh'Dar thought back to when he'd returned from Shadow Ridge with Kweeuu, riding almost entirely at night. How he'd occasionally stopped along the way for the wolf to eat a kill. He'd also worried himself sick then, so afraid that someone would spot and shoot the wolf. He remembered the relief he'd felt at approaching the Brothers' village with Kweeuu and imagined that the feeling would be even greater with his grandparents being involved.

Storm clouds rolled in as the journey continued, and a sharp breeze came up. *Those are definitely snow clouds*, Oh'Dar thought. *Snow flurries can't be far behind. If only we'd left a month ago.*

Another couple of days' travel and they'd be near the Webbs' village. From there, it was mostly open terrain and wilderness, but a significant leg of the journey was behind them.

※

Oh'Dar was right about the weather. Within a few hours, the skies had darkened, and heavy grey clouds seemed to press down, giving everything an ominous feel. Not too far ahead was the first river they had to cross. It was reasonably shallow, but he still stopped them before they reached it and explained.

"Ben, I know you've faced rivers before, and this isn't very deep, but this time it will be cold, so be sure to keep a tight hand on the reins."

Oh'Dar dismounted and walked up and down the bank, looking for the shallowest spot where he was sure the horses would be able to see the riverbed. When he found the right place, he mounted and rode Storm ahead of them to lead the way. As soon as Storm entered the water, he seemed to remember his previous crossings and relaxed. His lead calmed the other horses, and Ben was able to urge the wagon team on.

Slowly they made their way across the river. Once the wagon was safely on the other bank, Oh'Dar and Storm returned to fetch the other horses, which had been tethered to a tree on the opposite side. Luckily, they were also reassured by Storm's confidence, and Oh'Dar got them all safely across.

Unfortunately, they weren't as lucky when they came to the next river.

Oh'Dar surveyed the expanse of water before him. A breeze was kicking up spray, making the air colder, and the current was moving faster, all combining to be more unnerving for the horses. Beauty seemed agitated and pawed the ground. He looked over to see the wagon team already swishing their tails and tossing their heads nervously. The clouds had darkened even more, and he could smell rain in the air.

This time, Ben decided they should bring the spare horses over ahead of the wagon. He mounted Storm and led them all into the water. It took a little work to get the others going, but Storm's confidence seemed to reassure them. Then once again, Storm crossed the body of water without hesitation, which gave Oh'Dar an idea.

"Grandmother, why don't you take Storm; he isn't afraid of the water, and he'll cross more easily than the wagon. You've ridden him before, haven't you?" he asked.

"Only a few times. But I don't think he takes to me."

"She's right, Grayson. Storm really only accepts you and me," said Ben.

"Alright. Grandmother, stay on the wagon bench beside Ben and be sure to hang on tightly. I'll go ahead with Storm, and you follow with the wagon.

The current was strong, and the wagon started to angle sideways downriver. The team struggled to keep moving forward. They were almost clear when suddenly both horses stopped mid-stream. The current was too much for them.

Oh'Dar brought Storm back around. He watched helplessly as the water buffeted the wagon, worried that the current might start to carry it downstream, dragging the team with it. Not knowing what else to do, he jumped down off Storm and into the icy waters.

"Grayson!"

"I'm fine, Grandmother, just stay where you are, please," he called out. He moved to the left of the front horse and tugged on the bridle, encouraging it to move forward. Its eyes were wild with fear, and it was threatening to buck

"Vivian, sit down!" Ben called out to his wife, who had stood up to see if her grandson was alright. "Sit down!" he called out again, but Miss Vivian ignored him.

Just then, a clap of thunder broke out overhead, and the team startled, jerking the wagon forward.

Before Ben could react, Miss Vivian had been thrown into the icy water.

Oh'Dar turned around when he heard Ben frantically calling out. Hanging onto the reins for dear life, he looked to where Ben was pointing just as the team jerked the wagon across and onto the shore.

He quickly turned to see his grandmother a little way downstream, pulled down by the weight of her clothes and now partially submerged in the fast-moving current. Oh'Dar ran along the bank to get ahead of her and then plunged back into the cold waters. He managed to scoop her into his arms and struggled to pull her over to the bank, weighed down as she was by the soaked clothing. With Ben's help, he got her out of the torrent and onto the shore.

"Grandmother!" Oh'Dar patted her face and shook her gently. He could have cried when she finally opened her eyes.

He turned her over as she coughed up some water, "I'm so cold," she said, her voice wavering.

"Let's get her into the wagon," said Ben, and they lifted her and carried her to the back opening. Oh'Dar himself was soaking wet, but nothing mattered except taking care of his grandmother.

"We need her to get out of these wet clothes," Oh'Dar said. Then he hung his head, and turning away from Ben, broke down.

Ben jumped onto the wagon bed, in his desperation furiously opening one trunk after the other until he found some of Miss Vivian's clothing. He turned back with it bundled in his arms.

Once Miss Vivian had changed into her dry clothes, Oh'Dar brought some of the dry blankets over, and he and Ben wrapped her up as much as they could.

Oh'Dar pointed to a grove of trees on a higher ridge not too far away. "Let's try to find shelter there. I think I remember a rock outcropping that we could perhaps use as a windbreak if there are no other inhabitants since the last time I came through.

"Ha!" Ben snapped the reins on the wagon team and headed for the ridge; Oh'Dar on Storm was right behind him and the other horses.

Once Oh'Dar caught up to Ben, he rode on ahead and found the little cave he'd used on his trips back and forth. He tied up the horses and went in to inspect it, coming out fairly quickly and signaling that all was well. Ben pulled the wagon up as close as possible, then began unloading the dry blankets to make a spot for Miss Vivian.

Ignoring how cold he was himself, Oh'Dar immediately started gathering kindling and firewood. Once it was blazing, they moved Miss Vivian close and bundled her in extra blankets.

"It's a good thing you bought so many, son," Ben said as he furiously tried to rub warmth into his wife's hands.

"Best you get out of those wet clothes of yours, son," Ben urged Oh'Dar. Realizing for the first time how much he was shivering, and now that his grandmother was as safe and warm as they could manage, he could finally take care of himself.

"That's all we can do," said Ben. "Let's hope she doesn't get a chill. How far is it now to the Brothers' village?" he asked.

"Far," Oh'Dar said quietly. Then he turned to look at Ben. "We'll see how she is in the morning, but if she takes a turn for the worse, we may have no choice but to take her to the Webbs where she can recover inside, warm, and get some home-cooked food."

"They know your grandmother, right?"

Oh'Dar nodded, knowing Ben was referring to the attention they didn't want. "It can't be helped. Let's get her as warm and dry as possible. I'll make her some tea, and we'll sleep on either side of her tonight. In the morning, hopefully, she'll have recovered."

Oh'Dar added more wood to the fire until the flames seemed high enough to lick the sky.

Ben sat down next to his wife and wrapped his arms around her. He could feel her shivering, and he squeezed his eyes shut and hugged her tighter.

Oh'Dar went to check on the horses and covered them with some of the extra blankets. He was grateful they had so many.

That night, Ben slept up against Miss Vivian's back, and Oh'Dar slept in front of her, both using their body heat to keep her as warm as possible. Between the heat from the fire and the body heat trapped under the pile of blankets, her shivering finally stopped.

In the dark night, the tears Oh'Dar had held back finally slipped loose. *Please, Great Spirit. Please don't let my mistake, trying to cross the river, cost my grandmother her life.*

The next morning, Oh'Dar awoke to find Ben already up and another blazing fire going. His grandfather had heated some water to make his wife some tea. They helped her move to the fire, and once she was wrapped up tightly again, Ben gave her the tea to sip.

"This will warm you up inside."

Miss Vivian took the cup and wrapped her hands around it, warming her fingers.

"Thank you," she smiled at her husband. "I'll be fine; don't worry."

Oh'Dar came over from the wagon and handed her the last of the jerky. "Eat this, please."

She nodded and took it from him.

"As soon as you're warm, we're going to visit the Webbs," Oh'Dar announced.

"But Grayson—"

"Grandmother, please. You must be looked after. We still have a way to go, and you're in no condition to continue." He paused and knelt before her. "I'm sorry, Grandmother. I should never have—"

Miss Vivian hushed him, "Grayson, please stop right there. None of this is your fault." Just then, she gave a mighty sneeze and caught her grandson and her husband exchanging glances. "Alright. If you insist, we'll go to the Webbs." She tried to suppress the shivering that was threatening to start up again.

She watched, clutching her cup of tea, as Oh'Dar and Ben went about breaking up the camp, and finally, it was time. They helped her up and led her to the back of the wagon.

"Now lie down, and I'll make sure the blankets go all the way around and tuck under you," said Ben as he continued to fuss with making her comfortable. "You can rest and keep warm while we travel."

Oh'Dar had wrapped a towel around a warm rock

from the edge of the fire, and he placed it under the bottom of the blanket to warm her feet.

Miss Vivian grasped her grandson's hand as he tucked the coverings back. "Grayson, look at me," she said.

Oh'Dar stopped and met his grandmother's gaze before looking away.

"I'm going to be fine. You'll see. I haven't come this far in life to let a little dip do me in. Now go and finish what you were doing and let's be on our way. I promise I'll stay wrapped up," she said. She let go of his hand, and in jest, tipped down the brim of his hat.

"Alright then," said Oh'Dar.

Before long, she heard the snap of the reins and settled in for the balance of the ride. Her view from the back was of the horses walking behind, their beautiful coats gleaming in the sunlight, and the sound of the wagon wheels lulled her to sleep.

Oh'Dar led them through town, past the familiar buildings. They continued down the main street and then on to the Webbs' farm, which was down a winding dirt road not too far out. As they approached the house, he could see it was in a bit of a shambles. *I don't remember it being run down*, he thought, looking at the weeds that had grown up around the fencing. *Mr. Webb always kept the place up; I wonder what has happened?*

Oh'Dar dismounted, looped Storm's reins over a fence post, and ran up to the familiar modest farmhouse. He brusquely knocked at the door and waited, then knocked again and waited some more. He twirled around when he heard a familiar voice call out his name.

"Grayson!" It was Grace, and she hurried up to greet him, barely noticing the wagon that Ben had stopped some way away.

"Grace! Oh, my, look at you, how you've grown! Where's your mother?"

"She's back in the barn, come on!"

As they approached, Oh'Dar could see Mrs. Webb inside, mucking out the stalls. "Oh, Grayson," she exclaimed. "How good to see you!"

"Where's Mr. Webb?" he asked, surprised that she was undertaking such a task.

"There's so much to tell you, Grayson. This can wait; let's go inside and sit down for a bit!"

"I can't just yet, Mrs. Webb. I need your help," he said.

"Anything, Grayson, what is it? What's wrong?"

"My grandparents are with me. Well, my grandmother, Miss Vivian, who you'll remember, and her new husband, Ben, who you haven't met. But she took a spill in a river on the way here. I need a place for her to stay that's warm, where she can get her strength back. She's in the wagon, and I'm terribly worried she's caught a chill," Oh'Dar explained.

"Quickly, please, Grace, you come with me; let's prepare a room for them. Is Miss Vivian well enough to go upstairs?"

"I believe so," Oh'Dar answered.

"To be safe, we'll give her what has always been your room, Grayson," Mrs. Webb suggested. "Her husband can have Grace's room. Grace can bunk in with her father and me without a problem. Ned can sleep in the loft in the barn, where he sleeps most of the time anyway. Seems he'd rather be with animals than people any day."

Oh'Dar suppressed the urge to ask what was going on, knowing that the most important thing was to get his grandmother inside and that all the rest could be discussed later. Before long, introductions dispensed with, Mrs. Webb and Grace had Miss Vivian into a nice warm bed. She sighed with pleasure as she sank into the thick, soft mattress. Grace had gathered their warmest featherbeds and had her well tucked in before much time had passed.

Oh'Dar and Ben finally relaxed when, within moments, Miss Vivian was sound asleep. They sat around the kitchen table that was so familiar to Oh'Dar, and Mrs. Webb put dinner on the stove before joining them.

"A lot has happened since last you were here, Grayson," she said. "My husband took a fall a while ago and injured his back. It didn't heal properly, and he's often in a lot of pain. He's in town with Ned, seeing Dr. Miller and picking up some supplies. And as you can see, we haven't been able to keep the place up. Ned and Grace and I all do our best to get by."

Oh'Dar frowned as he listened to her woes, his heart heavy.

"You let us take care of your stables while we're here, ma'am," said Ben. "It's no trouble for us to do it, and I can see you need a rest. You look like you're at your wits' end, pardon my saying."

Mrs. Webb turned to hide her expression.

Oh'Dar reached across the table to get her attention. "Look at me, Mrs. Webb, please look at me," he said. "You aren't alone anymore. We'll help you. We will figure out how to help you," he said gently.

She broke down and sobbed, and Grace ran around the table to hug her mother. Little Buster sat quietly in the corner, watching, wagging his tail furiously each time anyone looked in his direction.

"Don't cry, Mama. You said help would come, and it did. Grayson and Mr. Jenkins will help us! It will get better, you'll see."

About that time, Mrs. Webb's husband and their son Ned came home.

"I didn't recognize the wagon out front nor the horses in the barn," Mr. Webb said as he pulled up a chair. "But by their quality, I should have known. I'm pleased to see you both." Oh'Dar averted his graze as the man lumbered into his seat, very obviously hobbled by his injury. Ned stood protectively behind his father.

"I guess my wife has told you about my accident," he said. "God bless her; she's doing the best she can around here. A bad stroke of luck, to be sure. But enough of me. Something smells good," he added, changing the subject.

Before long, Mrs. Webb served up a meager stew, supplemented with lots of bread and biscuits. There was no honey and very little butter, and later, as Mrs. Webb and Grace cleaned up and put things away, it was painfully apparent how barren the cupboards were.

After checking in on Miss Vivian, who was still sleeping soundly, Oh'Dar and Ben changed clothes and went off to finish mucking out the Webbs' barn. Oh'Dar insisted it was the least they could do to help pay for their keep.

As they worked, they talked quietly. "Things have really gone downhill here, Ben," said Oh'Dar. "This place was always pristine. I'm not glad for the accident that brought us here, but I am glad that I know they're in trouble. There must be something we can do to help the Webbs even though we can't stay here and take care of the manual labor. If they don't finish getting the crops in, they will starve for sure, and with barely enough for themselves, they won't have any extra with which to trade."

Suddenly, Oh'Dar's attention was caught by Grace standing in the doorway. "I came to tell you that your grandmother woke up and we gave her some food. She's resting again." Grace seized a pitchfork and joined them, but Oh'Dar leaned his against the wall and took it out of her hands.

"Hey!" she said, "I may be a girl, but I can help!"

"It has nothing to do with being a girl. This is backbreaking work, and you don't yet have the height or the strength for it. The last thing your mother needs is for you to get hurt."

"I have to find a way to help Mama some more," she hung her head. "I overheard them talking. The bank is going to take the house if we can't catch up on the mortgage."

"Mortgage?" asked Oh'Dar. "I didn't think your place was mortgaged?"

"Papa had to do it after he got hurt. The money lasted for a while, but now it's almost gone, and we can't pay the bank. I don't know what's going to happen to us."

Oh'Dar put down the pitchfork. "It's going to be alright, Grace. Ben and I will try to make sure you don't lose your home, I promise."

Then he rose back up and turned to Ben. "I'll be taking a trip into town tomorrow; if you want to come with me, you're welcome."

"Good for you, son. I might be more helpful

around here, though. These horses look like they need a good grooming, and I noticed the gate was hanging on one hinge."

Oh'Dar returned to working on the stalls while Grace practically ran back into the house to tell her mother the good news.

"I probably should have said something to Mr. Webb before saying that to Grace," Oh'Dar admitted.

"Hard for a man to take another man's charity," said Ben.

"They helped me first—when I needed it the most. I should go and talk to him if you don't mind." Ben nodded, and Oh'Dar went into the house to find Mr. Webb.

When he walked in, Grace was sitting down at the table with both her parents.

"I see Grace has told you that I want to help. I apologize, Mr. Webb. I should have talked to you first before running my mouth off like that.

"I appreciate the offer Grayson," said Mr. Webb. "But it's my problem to solve."

"Before you go any further, remember that you and your family extended yourselves to me first. You took me in at a time when I desperately needed a helping hand. I was a stranger in a foreign world with no friends and no idea what to do. If it weren't for your help, I'd never have found my grandmother. There's really nothing I can do that will repay you the kindnesses you showed me, so please at least let me do something. That's what family does."

Mr. Webb looked at Oh'Dar silently. Then he looked over at his wife.

"Just until you get on your feet again," Oh'Dar added.

Finally, Mr. Webb struggled to his feet and put out his hand, "I can't let the cost of my pride be my family's starvation, or my wife and children workin' themselves to death."

The two men shook on it.

"That's settled then. I'll be going into town with our wagon. Is there anything you need me to pick up?" Oh'Dar asked.

When no one answered, he added, "If you don't make a list, I'll just buy what I feel like."

Even the Webbs couldn't help but smile.

Grace looked at her mother, "May I go with Grayson? Please?"

"Alright, if he's taking the wagon, but then Ned must also go," said Mrs. Webb, to which Grace's face lit up.

Oh'Dar nodded, and Grace jumped up from her chair. He smiled, and together they went out to the barn to find Ned.

On the ride in, Oh'Dar asked Ned and Grace, "Does your mother let you go into the general store?

"Yes," Grace answered.

Oh'Dar reached into his pocket and handed them each some coins.

"Here. Go in and buy whatever you need. I saw your cupboards, and I want you to get everything you can think of. Now isn't the time to be frugal. And get some of those sugar sticks, if you would, for my grandmother. And also whatever treats your mother and father like. When we get there, I'm going to pull up and let you out, then I'll swing back around and pick you up again. If you need help when I return, ask the store owner to help you bring out whatever you've bought."

Grace tucked her coins into a little pocket on the front of her dress. Ned tucked his into his pants pocket.

Before long, Oh'Dar pulled up in front of the general store, and Ned and Grace dismounted and hurried inside. Then he snapped the reins and went on to make his other rounds, the wagon wheels leaving little trails in the dusty road that ran through the center of town.

The next morning, Oh'Dar went in to check on his grandmother. She turned her head and opened her eyes.

He smoothed her beautiful auburn hair away from her forehead. "You're burning up," he said. "When did this start?"

"I don't know. I just woke up cold. Can't seem to get warm enough."

Oh'Dar pulled the covers up and tucked them tightly under her. "I'll be back in a little while," he said.

He went back into the kitchen. "My grandmother has a fever. I'm going into town now, to fetch Dr. Brooks."

🐾

Oh'Dar, Ben, and the Webb family waited nervously for Dr. Brooks to come out of Miss Vivian's room. When he did, the solemn look on the doctor's face made Oh'Dar's heart sink.

"It isn't good, Mr. Jenkins. Your wife has quite a fever. It's a good thing you got her here when you did. She's where she needs to be, in bed with lots of care." He turned to Mrs. Webb. "Above all, keep her warm. If she tries to throw the covers off, don't let her. If the fever doesn't break, we could lose her."

Trying to maintain control, Oh'Dar tightened his jaw and clenched his fists while Ben nodded and thanked the doctor.

"I'll come back in the morning to check on her again," Dr. Brooks added.

"We'll do everything we can to take care of her, I promise," said Mrs. Webb, seeing Oh'Dar's tension.

"I know you will," Oh'Dar replied.

She then opened the wooden cupboard doors for

Oh'Dar to see inside. "I can't thank you enough. I don't remember them ever being this full."

He nodded. "If you can think of anything else you need, I can pick it up tomorrow when I go into town again. I'll probably go early as I've some other business to take care of and want to be back in time to see Dr. Brooks."

That night, Oh'Dar lay in an upstairs room with little Buster curled up behind his knees as usual. He tried to hold back his fears about his grandmother. To keep his mind occupied, he made a mental list of all the things he wanted to take care of. Since the doctor had said it might be weeks before his grandmother recovered, he knew he had more than enough time to put in place everything to make sure the Webbs had all the help they could possibly need.

※

The next morning found Oh'Dar, Ben, and Ned up early working in the barn. Between the three of them, they made some headway in getting things back in order. The Shadow Ridge horses seemed to enjoy being back in the familiar surroundings of a stall. While they were working, Ned explained that his father had fallen off a barn roof while helping some neighbors with their barn raising. It had taken him a long time to recover, during which they'd had no choice but to mortgage the property. Dr. Brooks said it was a miracle it didn't kill him.

Oh'Dar watched the young man work with the horses. "I hear you want to learn to doctor animals?"

"Yes. More than anything," Ned answered, continuing to work while he was talking. "Mr. Clement in town said he'd train me. But I can't start yet because of everything going on here. I have to be here to help Ma."

"When Mr. Clement retires, if I'm ready, he said I could take over his practice. I 'spect he probably has another ten or so years to work," Ned continued.

"Ned, do you know of any families around here who have sons who could use some work and have the time to do it?" Ben asked.

"What kind of work, sir?"

"Like we're doing here. The usual chores that go with keeping a homestead running."

"The Baxters at the next farm, they have seven sons. They might have the extra hands to help out. Should I tell you how to get there?" he asked.

"That would be very helpful, son," said Ben as he winked at Oh'Dar, who nodded back and mouthed *thank you.*

After they were done and cleaned up, Oh'Dar went to check on his grandmother. When he came in, she was awake and sitting up, having just eaten what Grace had brought her.

"Your wife must be worried that you've been gone so long," she said.

"How are you feeling?" Oh'Dar asked, pulling up a chair next to her bedside. He reached for her plate, and without thinking, set it on the floor. Buster came running over and made quick work of the egg and biscuit crumbs still on it.

"I'm tired, Grayson. It even tires me out to talk."

Oh'Dar took her hand in his. "You'll get better, and we'll be on our way before you know it. Just shut your eyes, and if you want, I'll tell you more about where we're going," he offered.

Miss Vivian nodded, so Oh'Dar told her more about his assignment to teach the children to speak and write English. He told her about the different ages and how many males and females they'd be working with. He explained how he used slate and chalk and taught them in the same way Miss Blain had taught him. He added that it would go better now he had the materials she'd used.

Oh'Dar thought she'd drifted off to sleep and got up to leave, but Miss Vivian opened her eyes and asked, "Do you not have paper? Ink and quills?"

Oh'Dar sat back down. "No. We don't have anything like that."

"They'd make it a lot easier," she said.

Oh'Dar was quiet for a moment. "I'm supposed to write down a history of the past. It was the other task my former Leader asked me to do. Having a written record that our people can access will preserve our history accurately from generation to generation. Having paper would make it a lot easier," he said.

"Do they have goats?" she asked, weakly lifting her head just a bit.

Oh'Dar chuckled. *I know where that's coming from. She's been enjoying the butter and cheese after being without it for so long. I hate to disappoint her, but—*

"No, and there's certainly enough brush and land for them to graze on, but the Brothers don't keep goats so I'm afraid it might draw undue attention." He looked at her with concern. "I can see you're tired; why don't you rest, and I'll check in on you later."

"Hmmm," Miss Vivian answered and rolled over onto her side. Oh'Dar tucked her in before quietly picking up the plate and leaving, Buster following alongside.

Oh'Dar washed the plate and put it up, all the while reflecting on what his grandmother had said. *Paper and quills. And ink, of course. No reason why we couldn't use that. It is a little expensive, but what other use do I have for all this money. And goats. I'd have to make a trip back for them and would probably have to order the paper, ink, and quills anyway. I don't think I want to add to this trip the trouble of transporting goats.*

Mrs. Webb came in just as he was finishing. "Grandmother is asleep again," he told her. "In the meantime, do you know anyone who has goats they might sell?"

"Goats? Well, probably. What do you need goats for?"

"Oh, just an idea Grandmother had, that's all," he answered. Mrs. Webb shrugged and started to set out what she needed to bake bread for the day. Oh'Dar didn't ask what had happened to the cow and goats they used to have, assuming they'd perhaps had to sell them, but their absence explained why they no longer had a good supply of milk and butter.

⚜

After letting Ben know what he was doing, Oh'Dar hooked the horses up to the wagon and set out for town. On the way, his mind was working over his grandmother's idea. *I wonder what else she might think of that would help everyone at the High Rocks. And the Brothers. Looks as if I might be making more trips back here than I'd expected.*

Oh'Dar pulled the team up to the bank and hopped out. He went inside and asked for the bank manager. A middle-aged man with round spectacles stepped out of a back office and beckoned Oh'Dar in. After they introduced themselves, Oh'Dar explained what he needed.

"I can take care of that for you, Mr. Morgan. I'd be happy to."

"Once my lawyer sends the paperwork, please make sure it gets to Mr. Webb and is signed properly. I have to put an order in at the general store, so I'll return sometime and fetch it from you. But it could be several weeks." Oh'Dar said.

"That won't be a problem. I'll get in touch with the right people, and we'll get everything taken care of. It's very generous of you, Mr. Morgan. The Webbs are fine people, and I can't tell you how it pains me to think of having to take their home and livelihood. You're an answer to prayer, that's for sure."

"Just doing what any decent person with the means would do. Thank you, sir, and good day," Oh'Dar got up, shook hands, and left the bank.

Next, he walked over to the general store. The storekeeper grinned widely on seeing him back so soon.

"What can I get for you today, Mr. Morgan?" he asked, wiping his hands on his apron.

"Nothing at the moment, though I'd like to place an order for some materials if you don't mind. Can you write down a list of what I need and see where you can get it from?"

"Sure can, but it might take a while, depending on what you need."

"It's not a problem. I'll pay for it all now and be back in a few months to get it. That is, if you have room to store what I need," Oh'Dar added.

"No matter, we'll make room, I assure you," said the storekeeper.

With business in town taken care of, Oh'Dar followed Ned's directions and went to visit the Baxters at the next farm over. Before too long, he'd made arrangements for three of the Baxter boys to help indefinitely with the Webbs' chores. After he left, he could tell the arrangement was mutually beneficial as the family looked as if they could use a little financial help themselves.

I'm glad that I'm in a position to help these fine people. Wealth is a great power. And a great responsibility; I can see that now. In the wrong hands, I imagine it can do great harm as opposed to good. Oh'Dar rode back to the Webbs with an easier mind. Having put in motion all he could think of to help them, his thoughts turned to prayer for his grandmother's full recovery.

By the time he got back, it was almost supper time. He washed up and sat down at the kitchen table. Grace had already taken a plate to his grandmother and reported that she'd eaten more than before and looked a little better.

As they passed the bowl of potatoes, the biscuits, butter, and stew around, Oh'Dar told them what he'd arranged for that day. Mr. Webb thanked him for arranging for the Baxters to help them. He said they were fine young lads, and with their help, he could probably spare Ned a day or so a week to begin studying with Mr. Clement. Everyone was in good spirits—better spirits than they'd been in a long time.

⁂

Over the next few weeks, Miss Vivian's health progressed steadily. In that time, Oh'Dar, Ben, and the neighbor lads had managed to get the Webb homestead back into good repair. Winter crops were planted, the farmland tilled, horses shoed and tended to, the fences repaired. By the time they were ready to leave and continue on their way, the Webb place and the Webb family had been transformed back to their former selves.

The morning they were preparing to leave, Oh'Dar had a favor to ask of Mr. Webb. "I hate to impose on you, but would it be possible to leave two of the horses until I can return for them? Dealing with the wagon team has proven to be a bit more than I anticipated. I can handle Beauty; I think it would be a comfort for my grandmother to have her with us. But we still have a way to go, and it would be a relief if I don't also have to worry about taking care of them."

"Certainly, Grayson," said Mr. Webb. "It's the least I can do for all your help; we'll keep them in the best of health, I promise. They're beautiful animals. What plans do you have for them?"

"I have some friends who will use them to improve their horses' bloodlines," Oh'Dar answered.

It was time for goodbyes. After a round of hugs, some tears, and heartfelt words, Oh'Dar mounted Storm. Ben and Miss Vivian were seated on the wagon bench, and the wagon itself was packed with supplies for the trip. They had kept part of the back clear in case Miss Vivian needed a break from sitting up front.

"Remember, you should be hearing from the bank manager about some notes to sign," Oh'Dar called out to the Webbs. "And I'll be back as soon as I can, weather permitting. Take care, and thank you for your hospitality."

As he and his grandparents pulled away, Oh'Dar briefly glanced back to take one last look at the people who had first taken him in and given him his place among the Waschini.

CHAPTER 3

T horak did his best to avoid returning to the Far High Hills. He was now a watcher and had asked for the farthest post out because he could not bear seeing Iella and Nootau together. *If they ever leave Amara, perhaps I will return to the community. But as long as they are here, it is better for everyone that I stay as far away as possible.*

With Thorak no longer the High Protector, Harak'Sar had promoted First Guard Dreth into the position. In time, the guards and watchers accepted the change, though morale took a hit from Thorak's failure to keep his personal feelings out of his professional duty. Having had a spotless record, it was a solemn reminder to everyone about the power of emotions and the need for balance between reason, will, and the heart.

Nootau and Iella settled into their life at the Far High Hills. Urilla Wuti continued her schooling with

Iella, indoctrinating her more and more in the special abilities that the older Healer had spent decades helping Adia develop. The more Urilla Wuti worked with Iella, the more impressed she was with her student's progression.

"You seem to be catching onto this very quickly. I do have to wonder if there is a genetic component after all," she mused one day after they had just finished a very fruitful session.

"If so, then the lifting of the ban against us pairing and having offspring should produce even stronger lines of Healers," Iella observed.

Urilla Wuti nodded as she wondered if, with both Iella and Nootau having healer bloodlines, their offspring might be doubly blessed with abilities. Only time would tell.

Harak'Sar and Khon'Tor were getting near the end of their morning meeting. "You have given me a great deal to think about," said the Leader of the Far High Hills.

Khon'Tor simply nodded in response.

"I would like you to start working with Brondin."

"Your first son?" Khon'Tor asked.

"Yes. I want you to mentor him. Spend time with him. Let him ask you questions about your experience as Leader at Kthama. If he asks you anything you do not wish to answer, just tell him so. I am sure you will have no problem doing that."

"Very well. Are you preparing to transition leadership to Brondin?"

"Not anytime soon. But one never knows. He is still too young to take over, but he has expressed an interest and I would prefer to foster it. As for my other sons—they, fortunately, do not wish to lead."

"Fortunately?" Khon'Tor asked.

"It makes it less difficult when there are no hard feelings between siblings. Their interests lie in other directions."

"I see."

"You and I are cut from the same cloth, Khon'Tor. We are both demanding Leaders. Others have their own way, but I have always felt a kindred spirit in you."

"Harak'Sar—" Khon'Tor started.

The Leader raised his hand to interrupt, "You must let the sins of the past go; I see the shame in you every time we speak. Punishment has been delivered. If you still seek redemption, find it by bringing your gifts to the community to help us weather the difficult future that is no doubt ahead of us."

Harak'Sar got up and pushed the meeting room boulder in place, sealing the room against his next question being overheard.

"You have seen the offspring of Adia the Healer and High Protector Acaraho," Harak'Sar said.

"He is no longer High Protector; he is the Leader of the High Rocks. But yes, I have."

"Clearly, the offspring is an aberration. There is no natural explanation for an offspring to be born like that. Whatever his coming heralds, it will not be an easy path. Yes, I know the People are comforted by the Sarnonn proclamation that he will bring in a new age. But you and I both know that peace is often hard-won on the tails of much conflict. To think otherwise is folly. And we are not people of folly, are we?"

Khon'Tor nodded, admitting he had entertained such thoughts himself. "I share your concerns. I have not spoken of it to anyone, lest it appear petty on my part. As if I begrudge Acaraho the happiness he has found in having a son, and the honor of leading Kthama."

"Whatever is coming, it is not going to be a gentle stroll into the welcoming arms of peace and plenty. Those of us who realize this must do what we can, silently in the background, to prepare for the hard times to come. Perhaps harder times than we have ever experienced before."

"I appreciate your candor," Khon'Tor said.

"Good. Then let us dismiss. I shall let Brondin know that his training will begin with you on your schedule. Anyone can send him to you when you are ready."

Harak'Sar got up to remove the boulder.

"Wait," said Khon'Tor.

Harak'Sar turned and looked back.

"There is more I must know. If you and I are to act as equals, as counsel to each other, I must know the truth. What happened that Urilla Wuti is now Overseer? What has become of Kurak'Kahn?"

"Kurak'Kahn intended to murder you. The whip he used was a Jhorallax. A weapon banned long ago, as you know, for being too brutal and deadly. I am certain that no one still alive has ever seen one. When the Healers tended to you, they found the shards left by the whip buried deep in your flesh. It was that which brought on the infection. Acaraho figured it out and confronted Kurak'Kahn, who admitted that he wanted you dead."

Khon'Tor stared at Harak'Sar and finally asked, "But why?"

"Kurak'Kahn claimed that the unknown victim you raped, the one who never came forward and whom you could not identify, was his niece. She bore an offspring at about the right time. Her mate accused her of being unfaithful and did not believe her story of being Taken Without Consent. In the end, he physically attacked her and abducted the child. Kurak'Kahn said that his niece, unable to bear the pain of it, had thrown herself from a high cliff and ended her life. For this, he blamed you."

Khon'Tor had to look away. When he glanced back, he said, "It could well be true. It could well have been my fault that she is dead now and the offspring is missing. I assume they did not see any evidence of the offspring's—" His voice trailed off.

"The offspring's body? No. It could be that these events were put in place by you. But we will never know. However, using his position as cover, that was Kurak'Kahn's motivation for trying to murder you. When you came forward and confessed of your own accord, it played right into his hands."

"And what buys his silence?"

"Acaraho made a deal with him that he was to say nothing lest he be prosecuted for his crime against you and for the abuse of his station."

"And who knows of this?" Khon'Tor asked.

"Acaraho, Adia, the Healer, her Helper Nadiwani, Urilla Wuti, Risik'Tar, and Lesharo'Mok. And, of course, Kurak'Kahn. Whether his mate, Larara, knows or not, depends on whether he told her the truth about his own part in it. Which I doubt. If it was this female whom you took Without Her Consent, then that is what is on your soul. What happened between her and her mate thereafter was not your doing," Harak'Sar continued.

"But I set the events in motion. And now many more lives are ruined," Khon'Tor said. Then he added, "Thank you for telling me the truth."

"There is more. Acaraho and I committed to sending our people out to look for the offspring or any signs or clues about what might have happened to him. I admit now that I have been remiss in following through. I need to rectify that."

Her session with Urilla Wuti finished, Iella went to find Nootau. He was working outside in the fields, planting with Hollia, which seemed to be one of his favorite pastimes.

"I have never known anyone to love plants and the Great Mother's creation as you do," she said as she approached.

He looked up from his toil and smiled. "Only surpassed by my love for you, Saraste'" he said. "Here." He held out a creamy-white lace-dancer bloom that she took and tucked into her hair above one ear.

"I am done with my work with Urilla Wuti this morning," she explained. "I thought we might spend the day together."

"What did you have in mind?" he asked, a twinkle in his eye.

She laughed, "Well, that, yes, but later. I would like to go to the caves down past the bend in the river and see if we can find any more fluorite."

"I will be done here in a little while. I will find a carrying basket and meet you there if you wish to get a head start."

Iella made her way down the river bank, enjoying the feel of sunlight on her face. The cold breeze coming up across the water made the slight warmth of the sun even more enjoyable. She picked her way along the water's edge, careful not to cut her foot coverings on the sharper rocks and shells.

She found the opening to the cave and entered. The moment she was there, she knew she had made a terrible mistake.

She was face-to-face with a huge brown bear, its fangs open in a terrifying snarl. The People had few encounters with bears, ordinarily giving them the respect they deserved and staying out of their way. Nowhere as dangerous as a Sarius snake, the males of the People could kill one if needed. Still, they were loath to take the life of any living creature other than for food, and bears were revered by the Brothers as fellow healers who represented the love of the Great Mother.

Not daring to avert her gaze from the bear, out of the corner of her eye, she saw movement. Peeking out from behind were two cubs. *Oh no*, she thought, *a mother bear. The one thing possibly as dangerous as a Sarius snake, and I am unarmed.*

The bear shook its head, then rose on its hind legs. Letting out a piercing roar, it shook its head, fur flinging around as if in slow motion. Iella saw her life with Nootau ripped apart before her in a flash.

She felt the fear rising in her gut. Knowing there was only one power that could help her, she closed her eyes. She prayed to the Great Mother and calmed herself. When moments had passed and the attack still had not come, she opened her eyes. The bear was still standing, just looking at her, and the cubs had wandered farther behind it.

Something moved deep inside Iella, and she held up her palms, saying calmly, "Let there be peace between us, Honawmato; I mean you and your offspring no harm."

The bear continued to stare at Iella before dropping back to all fours. Much to Iella's amazement, the giant creature shook itself all over, then slowly turned and led her cubs farther back into the recesses of the cave. The little brown bodies scampered clumsily after their mother's giant, shaggy form.

Iella did not move. She barely blinked. Then, gathering herself, she slowly backed out of the cave and inched her way back to the riverbank.

In the distance, she could see Nootau coming her way. She waved her arms, palms facing him, and he stopped where he was.

Her heart racing, Iella made her way toward Nootau as quietly as possible. When she reached him, she said, "Come. We must turn back; in the cave is a mother bear with her cubs."

"What!" he said. He immediately looked his mate up and down in case she had any injuries.

"I am fine. I will tell you about it later; please, let us leave."

Nootau put his arm around her shoulder and led

her back to the safety of Amara's walls while she told him what she had just experienced.

Once inside, he led Iella to the eating area and had her sit down. Then he came back with a calming drink in a little gourd. He had asked one of the females there please to fetch Urilla Wuti, who soon joined them.

Nootau explained to the older Healer what had happened.

"I know better than to walk into a cave without thinking," Iella said. "It was a foolish mistake. But what was peculiar is that the bear seemed to understand me when I called it by name and said I meant it no harm."

She took a sip from the gourd. "I have not had an experience like that before. Have you?" she asked her aunt.

"No. But it seems many things are changing. Your abilities are progressing at a rate I have not seen before, not even with Adia of the High Rocks. Perhaps this is caused by more of your abilities coming to the fore. Though I do not suggest that you intentionally test your ability to communicate with the Great Mother's creatures. At least, not any that size," said Urilla Wuti.

"That is a good point," said Nootau. "I think you *should* test them. We could go out and see if you can communicate with the smaller animals. It is worth a try. I do not know where this might lead, but it is an interesting turn of events. It seems a little like the way in which all the creatures are drawn to An'Kru."

"It does. I wonder if it has anything to do with him?" Iella pondered. Then she leaned in and rested her head on Nootau's shoulder.

"I do not know what I would do if anything happened to you," he said softly.

Urilla Wuti looked at them sitting together. Something in Nootau had changed. Somehow, he suddenly seemed so much more mature. Had something happened to him? Or was it just more of the effect that E'ranale had said An'Kru would bring— the widening between good and evil, the augmentation of who they were at their core.

Curious to experiment, Iella went for a walk down the paths that wound everywhere around Amara. The brisk air brought her the scent of deer, squirrel, raccoon, and the rich loam of the forest floor. She found a quiet area, one of her favorites, ringed by tall lush ferns and through which a little stream meandered. Iella made herself comfortable on a fallen log, her feet dangling inches above the slow-moving water. The songbirds' lilting calls broke the silence, and the afternoon sunlight breaking through the treetops completed the idyllic scene. Iella could not have imagined a more peaceful and beautiful setting.

She focused on her breathing and did as Urilla

Wuti had taught, slowing her inner vibration until she felt in harmony with the stillness about her. Then she reached out her mind to see if she could feel any other living creatures nearby.

After a few moments, Iella opened her eyes and looked around but did not see any of the creatures that, by their scent, she knew to be in the area. Trying again, this time she quieted the tyranny of her thoughts and simply focused on what she could sense around her. The sweet smell of the forest floor, the quiet rippling of the water trickling past, the reeds and tall grasses tickling her feet. In the quietness of herself, she realized how content she was. And suddenly, she had company.

She opened her eyes to see a little grey squirrel perched on a branch close to her. He tipped his head as if looking her over. Iella was filled with a surge of love for this little creature. She saw how perfect he was, his variegated grey hairs that overlapped each other, his tiny little claws in his paws, which were curled up in front of him. And for a moment, she saw life through his eyes. The vastness of the forest, the soothing, protective cover of the tall plants, the slow wordless rhythm of life. Her sense of the little creature began to deepen, and it felt almost as if she was the little squirrel. She could feel the satisfaction of his solid purchase on the tree branch—the secure grip of his hind feet around the bark, the slight swaying of the tiny branch under its weight as it shifted. She felt the warmth of the little shaft of light that peeked through the leaves over-head and warmed his back—the counterweight of his tail keeping his balance without effort or thought.

For a short while, Iella was transmuted into a life lived in each moment, whether it be a joyful bounce from limb to limb, the happy discovery of a newly fallen acorn, the fresh burst of a ripe berry in his little mouth, the morning blessing of fresh dew drops on the leaves. She felt his instinct to gather and bury, to prepare for the winter. It was a stirring, an urging, not below the surface but coursing through his very body. Wordless knowing; *the time is now. Do not tarry in your tasks.*

Suddenly the snap of a twig startled them both, and the connection was broken. The little squirrel scurried off as fast as he could.

Iella looked up to see that Nootau had found her. "I am sorry, am I interrupting?"

She smiled at her mate, but instead of returning it, he peered at her strangely. "Is something wrong? You had a peculiar look on your face when I came up."

"Oh. An odd experience. Not sure I can explain it. There was a little grey squirrel here. And I seemed to fall into such a state of affinity with him that it became hard to tell our minds apart. I think this must be related to what happened with Honawmato, the bear at the cave."

"Whatever it is, I see no harm in it. It seems to me

it can only turn out to be a great gift," Nootau said, sitting down next to her.

"I am anxious to tell Urilla Wuti about it. Perhaps she will be able to teach me how to hone it. It was truly a pleasant experience, being a fat little squirrel."

Nootau smiled. "I am sure there are also times when it is not pleasant to be a fat little squirrel."

Iella raised her eyebrows. "Sadly, you are right." Then she asked him, "How is your work with Urilla Wuti coming on?"

"I am not really sure. My dreams with the Guardian, Pan, and with An'Kru, seem to come unbidden."

"What?" she gasped. "An'Kru? What are you talking about?"

"It was just like the experience I had with Pan, in a place that defies description. Only, instead of Pan, I met An'Kru. He was a grown male, and he told me not to worry about my role in taking care of him. He told me to enjoy my life with you and trust that everything was working out as it should."

Iella frowned, concentrating on his every word.

"I will tell you, I never wanted to leave his side. I cannot explain what it was like being in his presence."

"Does your mother know of this?" Iella asked.

Nootau let out a huge sigh. "No, I never did say anything to her. It happened at a time when I was particularly upset about us. Wanting to be with you, yet concerned I would not fulfill my duty by An'Kru. I must tell her as soon as I see her next."

"I think you should tell Urilla Wuti too, if you have not."

"Do you want to go and find Urilla Wuti now? It seems we both have stories to tell," said Nootau.

Urilla Wuti listened silently as Iella and Nootau told their stories. When they had both finished, she sat quietly for a while. They knew she was thinking, pondering, considering, and they honored her silence.

Finally, she spoke. "Ever since the opening of Kthama Minor, there has been a shift in the supernatural plane. If we could talk to the Healer community, I believe we would hear more stories such as these. At the next High Council meeting, I will hold a separate conference of the Healers and Helpers. I do not have answers at present, but I suspect they are ours to discover collectively and individually as the intent of what is unfolding becomes made known."

She rose, signaling the end of the meeting. "In the meantime, of course, I wish to continue my work with each of you."

"But," said Nootau. "I do not think what is happening to me has anything to do with me. I do not see it as any ability such as Iella is experiencing.

The messages just come; they are not a power or a skill I can control."

"I am not convinced of that," said Urilla Wuti. "Oh, it may turn out to be true that you cannot force the messages to come, but I suspect you can enhance your ability to receive them. In each instance, the information you were given turned out in some way to be pivotal."

Nootau nodded, stood, and reached out his hand to help Iella to her feet. "Thank you. We will leave you now to your other work."

Tehya had just finished preparing a meal when Khon'Tor found his way back to their quarters.

"I did not find you in the eating area, so I thought perhaps you might wish to eat here," she said.

He nodded and went over to inspect the meal. "You have gathered my favorite things."

"Come; sit down and tell me about your day. I saw you speaking with Harak'Sar."

Khon'Tor sat down before speaking. "We discussed what the future might hold."

Tehya started picking at her food as she sat patiently, waiting for him to continue.

"And he told me something disturbing. Kurak'Kahn claims that the third female I attacked was his niece. She asked to be paired directly after the Ashwea Awhidi at which I violated her. He said she bore a child who did not resemble her mate, Berak, who then accused her of being unfaithful. She told Berak she had been Taken Without Consent, but he did not believe her. Instead, he turned violent and hurt her. Later, the mate abducted the offspring, a male, and left the community."

Tehya abandoned her food and turned her attention fully to her mate. "How terrible for her. Please tell me the offspring has been recovered."

Khon'Tor shook his head. "No. They searched and found no sign of him—but they are a small community with few resources. And there is more. The female's body was found at the bottom of a ravine. It is not known if she took her own life or if her mate had something to do with it. Or it could have been an accident. But they said he had struck her before in an argument over the offspring."

"So that explains Kurak'Kahn's hatred; he blames you."

"He and I; we both do," he answered.

Tehya squeezed back the tears that were threatening to spill for her tortured mate. "I cannot release you from the prison of your self-condemnation. But if there is something—anything—I can do, please tell me what it is, and I will do it."

Khon'Tor got up and walked away from her. "I need to search for the offspring."

Tehya looked at him. *In body, he is still the robust and virile male I paired with, but the spark is gone from his spirit.* "Alone?"

He turned back to face her. "The Leaders pledged to send people from our communities to look for any sign of what happened to him. No, I would not be going alone."

"Whatever you need to do. Do not worry about leaving me; I will be safe here. Akar'Tor is no more. My parents are here, and my brothers are in from their watch cycle. Arismae and I will be waiting for you when you return."

Khon'Tor shook his head, "I have no idea of where to begin. They do not know where the offspring was taken. No one knows if he is even alive."

"If you feel called to do this, then you must. I believe the guidance will come," said Tehya firmly. *Perhaps this will give his soul rest. I do not want him to go, but he cannot continue like this, filled with remorse and self-hate. Nothing seems to lift the burden from his soul, not even the horrific whipping the Overseer inflicted at Kayah's request.* "Perhaps the Overseer—perhaps Kurak'Kahn has more details he could give you. If you approached him yourself?"

"Let us hope his desire to recover the offspring is stronger than his hatred for me. I will go to him as you suggest. Now, please eat. No more talk of this type; rather tell me what you have been doing."

Tehya tried to set the matter from her mind as she told Khon'Tor about her day with her friends, Arismae, and her parents. She told him she had started thinking again about designing wraps for the females and now, due to Nootau's lead in adopting coverings, also had the males to consider. As she chatted on, she kept watching him and hoped she was helping to take his mind off his troubles.

Later, when they turned in, she could sense that sleep was evading him.

❀

A few days later, Khon'Tor told Harak'Sar he was willing to take a group of males and start the search for U'Kail. But he would need to visit Kurak'Kahn first to see if there was any information not yet disclosed that might help them narrow down the search area. Realizing the priority of that commitment, Harak'Sar decided that Brondin's training with Khon'Tor could wait until the mission was completed.

"Take care, Khon'Tor," Harak'Sar warned. "Acaraho made a deal with Kurak'Kahn for his silence, but that did not change the former Overseer's hatred of you. We did commit to providing help to find the child, and before you go, I will gather some males for the search as I promised I would do."

❀

Khon'Tor and Tehya shared a tender good-bye. Not knowing how long he would be gone, he studied her face for a while, gently kissed her fingertips, and promised to return safely.

With three of Harak'Sar's best watchers and three of his guards, Khon'Tor set out for the community of the former Overseer. Knowing they would be out in the elements for an extended period, they had donned foot coverings and wraps. They also carried spears and had sharpened blades in their satchels. Though they had dried foodstuffs, they would need to hunt while they were away.

Their arrival was met with surprise as the little community did not often have visitors. They were all left waiting in the small entrance for Kurak'Kahn to appear. Time passed, and then, finally, Kurak'Kahn's mate, Larara, arrived instead.

"Welcome, Khon'Tor." She nodded to the others. "I am sorry, but my mate says he is not feeling well and is not up to seeing you. I felt it rude not to offer an explanation. Would you like something to eat after your journey here?"

"Perhaps in a while," Khon'Tor said, and the other males nodded their agreement. "I will be quick in telling you why we are here. We have come to search for the offspring of your niece, Linoi. I have heard the story as relayed by your mate but wanted to speak with you both first-hand to see if there might be any details of his disappearance that were overlooked."

Larara let out a long sigh. "I will tell you all I can, but I do not believe it will be enough to go on. Berak could have taken U'Kail anywhere, and so much time has passed. But in case there is any hope, of course, come let us sit down."

Larara led them farther inside and told them everything she could. When she was done, Khon'Tor asked about Berak's background.

"His family has been part of our community for generations. His parents, grandparents, are all here."

"Would they be willing to speak with me?" Khon'Tor asked.

Larara nodded and left. Before too long, she returned with Berak's parents. She introduced them and then deferred to Khon'Tor, who led the conversation.

He explained why he was there and asked them if they had any thoughts about where Berak might have gone.

His mother spoke up, "Berak's life was here, with us. And with Linoi. I still cannot accept that he harmed her. But I saw her wounds, so I have to believe that he did. I know you all suspect he harmed U'Kail, but I do not believe so. As for where he would go, the only thing I can think of is that his mother's sister was paired with a male at the Far Flats. But that is so far away. They are an isolated community, and I do not believe the People around here have ever had any contact with them. Do you think he could have taken the offspring there?"

"Based on his crimes, I suspect it. He would not be able to go to any of our local communities, as word of his identity would get through," said Khon'Tor.

In the end, other than the statement about his possible tie to the Far Flats community, there was not much more than Khon'Tor already knew. But he thanked them, and then he and the other males took Larara up on the meal and an overnight stay.

In the morning, as the group was preparing to head out, Larara came to wish them well. "Where will you search?" she asked.

"We discussed it after we met with you," Khon'Tor replied. "We are in agreement that he most likely headed for the Far Flats. We are going to search in that direction."

"It will take you a while to get there," she said, though not wanting to sound ungrateful or discourage them from their decision. "And there are so many routes Berak could have taken."

"I know. But we will head there, and if we find any signs, we will decide whether or not to continue and send for reinforcements and supplies. Harak'Sar has assigned his best men, those who are the most sensitive to the magnetic lines. Since all our communities lie along those, once we pick up the current, we should be on the same path that Berak took."

What Khon'Tor did not say, but what everyone knew, was that if Berak had not prepared for the journey before he left, there was little hope of his survival. The People did not do well separated from the communities, so banishment was usually a death sentence.

Larara thanked them and bade them farewell as Khon'Tor led the group of Harak'Sar's males on the start of their journey in the direction of the Far Flats.

She returned to their quarters and addressed her mate, who was sitting in the eating area. "I still do not know why you would not speak with them. They were here to help. You could at least have come and greeted them. I cannot give up hope as you have. I cannot bear to believe he is gone forever."

Kurak'Kahn did not look up from his seat.

"What I do not understand," she continued, "is why you seem to resent Khon'Tor so. You would not help when that Kahrok came looking for him. You said you did not care about Khon'Tor and had washed your hands of anything to do with Kthama. And here is this group of strangers, led by the renowned Khon'Tor himself, all willing to leave their families and loved ones to try and find our grandson. What is it you are not telling me?"

Kurak'Kahn did not look at her, nor did he answer. After a while, still with no response, Larara turned and left.

Khon'Tor and the males set out in the direction of the Far Flats. The watchers would play a critical role in identifying the magnetic currents and helping them navigate both there and back. The energy vortexes were connected like a web or a series of tributaries in a river system. Since the opening of Kthama Minor—Kht'shWea—even the more subtle currents that, before, had been undetectable to them were now noticeable. Combining the watcher's sensitivities with their knowledge of the current that snaked toward the Far Flats, they walked together in silence, looking for any sign of previous travel. It had not much chance of success, as it was some time since Berak had taken the offspring. But they were committed to trying, so they carried on without complaint. Despite the cold and the slim chance of success, it still gave Khon'Tor a sense of purpose, and for that, he was grateful.

Back at the Far High Hills, Tehya had set up a little work area in one of the empty rooms Harak'Sar had graciously let her take over. Much as in Oh'Dar's workshop at Kthama, she and her friends would gather and discuss different ways of securing their wraps, trying to come up with new ideas. She regretted never reminding Oh'Dar to model his Waschini clothes for her when she was at Kthama. After seeing the Waschini weapon, she was sure they must have innovative clothing that she could somehow copy—if she could just get a look at it.

Tehya's mother, Vosha, had joined them that day and was watching Arismae so Tehya could concentrate on the different hides and materials and chat with her friends, uninterrupted.

"So where is that mate of yours?" asked Dostah.

Tehya remembered that Dostah was the female who had earlier tried to reach out and touch Khon'-Tor's wraps after making complimentary statements about how he looked in them. Trying not to frown, she answered, "He is away on a mission for a while. I am not sure when he will return."

"You must miss having him in your bed then," Dostah twittered. "I know I would."

Tehya could feel her mother watching her and knew that Vosha could tell she was upset by Dostah's remarks. But the comment did make Tehya think back to the last time she and Khon'Tor had mated, which was just before he left. Knowing it would be a while before they were together again, he had taken her more than once that night, and each time filled her to satisfaction.

Vosha tried to help by refocusing the group on the designs. "Go back a few to that dark piece," she said to Tehya, who flipped the stack of materials back to a particularly dark hide. "You should set that piece aside and see if Iella might be interested in making some new wraps for Nootau. That would match his dark coloring beautifully," Vosha said.

"I will ask her now that you thought of it," Tehya answered.

After a while, the talk died down, and Tehya's friends left one by one.

After the others had all left, Vosha stayed to talk to her daughter. "I am glad you have the company of other females again. But why are you letting Dostah get to you?" she asked.

Tehya rubbed her hand over her face. "Ever since we were little, I felt that she competed with me. We were friends, so I overlooked it. But now, it seems harder to do. I do not know if I am just more sensitive, or if she is bolder about it," Tehya explained. "I do not know how to put it; it just seems as if everyone is more—either nicer and kinder, or going the other way to be less nice and less kind. I will try better to ignore it, Mama. I know it is important to get along with others."

Vosha handed Arismae back to her. "Here, let us get you settled back in your quarters. I think you could use some company now that Khon'Tor is away. Shall we sit up and chat like we used to when you were growing up?" Tehya nodded and tucked Arismae into the sling. *Mother is right; I do miss Khon'Tor so much. And I am very tired of the drama; it has been nonstop for so long. I just want everything to settle down. Perhaps when he returns, we can find our routine here and focus on being content.*

CHAPTER 4

The rest of the travel toward the Brothers' village was happily uneventful. With his grandmother fully recovered, Oh'Dar concentrated on keeping from the usual route to avoid any other travelers, however unlikely. He was cautious not to go so far out of the way that he got them lost, however. They made frequent stops, as saddles and the hard wagon seat had their limits comfort-wise.

Each evening when they made camp, he took pleasure from hearing his grandparents talking between themselves as he cared for the horses. He was anxious to get to the village but wanted them to arrive as rested and as healthy as possible; he knew that emotions would run high once they arrived and the strangeness of everything hit them. When she was not looking, he studied his grandmother for any sign of weariness.

One evening, the horses cared for, Oh'Dar finally joined them at the fire. When he sat down, his grandmother draped a blanket around his shoulders.

"How much farther do you think?" she asked as she patted it around him.

"Based on our rate of travel, I believe about four more days."

"Oh, Ben, I'm a little frightened now that it's all becoming real," she exclaimed, sitting next to her husband and resting her head on his shoulder.

The stars sparkled in the dark night sky overhead. Oh'Dar stretched out on his back so he could look up at them. Without thinking, he started tracing the patterns his father had taught him and named them to himself. The cold night air bit at his nose. He could hear the yipping of coyotes in the distance beyond the backdrop of the crackling fire.

Ben had insisted on bringing his rifle. Hearing the coyotes a little closer than he would have preferred, Oh'Dar was grateful that Ben had it handy.

Oh'Dar saw his grandmother look around nervously. "I will be glad when we're indoors again," she said.

"Why don't you sleep in the wagon tonight, if that would make you feel safer?" Oh'Dar asked. "And yes, you won't feel so vulnerable once we get to the Brothers' village. For one thing, there will be many people there, and that will bring you comfort, I'm sure."

"We won't be able to understand them," Miss Vivian pointed out to him.

"No. But the People do have a hand sign language, and we can work on that. Also, my wife, her siblings, and her mother, Honovi, speak English. Honovi's mother was married to a white man."

"So your wife is partly white?" his grandmother asked.

"Yes, and she probably understands even more English than she can speak. But Honovi was raised mostly in the village, so she has no experience of your world." Oh'Dar sat up and moved closer to the fire. "Please don't worry, Grandmother, the horses will warn us if there's any trouble from the coyotes."

"Grayson is right, Vivian," interjected Ben. "There's far easier game out here for them than us. But I think we should turn in. No doubt the upcoming days are going to be taxing."

In the end, both Ben and Miss Vivian decided to sleep in the wagon, up off the ground and buried under a mountain of blankets. Oh'Dar smothered the fire and enjoyed the heat radiating from the stones he'd banked it with.

Before long, it was morning again—time to tend to the horses and get back on their way.

The next four days passed without incident. Oh'Dar breathed a sigh of relief when he first saw the familiar landscape of the Brothers' territory. He knew that before long, the scouts would spot them and take back word of his return.

Acise and her sister came walking into the village, bundles of twigs and sticks for the fire in their arms. They chatted happily as they walked, kicking up clumps of dead leaves and disturbing the dusting of snow on the ground ahead of them. As they stopped to drop off their gatherings, they heard the rapid hoofbeats of someone riding in haste.

"Oh'Dar is returning! Oh'Dar is returning!" shouted the young brave. He pulled his pony to a halt and dismounted in a hurry. Acise ran toward him, her skirt whipping around her hide boots.

"Where? How far away?"

"Close. I will run and tell Chief Is'Taqa!" and the man took off, running toward the Chief's shelter.

Before long, everyone was gathered at the far end of the village from which direction the travelers were expected. Finally, over the hill appeared the wagon, pulled by a beautiful team of sturdy horses, with Oh'Dar in the lead on Storm.

Some of the children started to run toward the wagon, but the littlest ones were quickly snatched up by their parents. Slowly the group came close enough for the Brothers to see that, indeed, there were two older Waschini in the wagon.

Oh'Dar brought Storm in and quickly dismounted. Within moments, Acise was in his arms, and they clasped each other tightly. "I have missed you so," she whispered into his ear. "And I have missed you," Oh'Dar said, nuzzling her neck and squeezing her tighter. He released her and led her back to the wagon, which had come to a halt a few feet back.

Oh'Dar introduced his grandmother first, before turning to Ben. Both children and adults could not help staring curiously at Miss Vivian's hair coloring.

She smiled warmly at Acise. "I'm so happy to meet you. My grandson has told us how much he loves you."

Oh'Dar helped her from the wagon as Ben jumped down from the other side. Just then, the crowd parted as Chief Is'Taqa and Honovi came forward.

Miss Vivian looked at the magnificent Chief standing before her. His long straight black hair; his eyes shining with wisdom; his natural hide clothing that made him look as much a part of nature as everything surrounding them. He nodded to her and said something which she assumed was a welcome.

Then Oh'Dar introduced them to the woman standing next to the Chief.

She smiled and said, "We welcome you to our village. I am Honovi, wife to Chief Is'Taqa, and mother of Oh'Dar's wife, Acise." She indicated the beautiful young woman still standing next to Oh'Dar. "We have been waiting for you. Come, let us make you comfortable."

Miss Vivian looked at her grandson, who nodded his encouragement.

"I'll bring the wagon around, and we'll offload your things in a few moments," he said.

Two braves volunteered to take care of the horses, so Ben took his wife's arm, and as they walked, a parade of children followed along beside them. Miss Vivian could not help but keep looking down at them and smiling. The smell of cooking fires brushed her senses, and the cold air stung her face.

Honovi led them to what looked like a brand-new construction. "This is the place belonging to my daughter and your grand—grandson." She stumbled a bit before finding the correct word. "You will have privacy here and can rest as much as you wish."

As Honovi held the flap open, Miss Vivian and Ben stooped down to enter. Once inside, they straightened up and looked around. It was sparse yet welcoming. The sloping walls were made of wood lashed together and covered with stretched hides. The ground had been swept clear, with several colorful blankets and animal hides scattered about. In the center was a fire pit and light shone in from above around the edges of the covered smoke hole.

Acise and Oh'Dar followed them in.

"It's very cozy," Miss Vivian observed.

Oh'Dar showed them how the flap at the top of the shelter let the smoke out when there was a fire going inside. "Why don't you and Ben sit down. I'll bring some of your blankets in here, and you can wrap up until I can get a fire going."

Miss Vivian nodded and suddenly felt all the

wear and tear of the journey closing in on her. She asked which mats they should use, and Oh'Dar showed her two newer-looking ones. When she sat down, she realized they were softer than she had thought, with soft gatherings of leaves and grasses beneath.

Comforted by the welcome feeling of enclosure, Miss Vivian started to cry.

Ben wrapped his arms around her and pulled her into him. "Oh no, what's wrong? Tell me please," he begged her.

"I'm so tired. And I didn't realize until now just how much I missed being *inside*," Miss Vivian answered, her voice muffled by his embrace.

"We'll stay inside here as long as you wish. These people seem to be very understanding. You need to rest and get something warm to eat. Things will seem better after a few days," he comforted her.

Just then, Honovi entered with a wooden bowl in her hands. When she saw the tears in Miss Vivian's eyes, she moved quickly to kneel down in front of her.

"You are tired. It must be very hard, leaving everything you know. Here, this will help you feel better."

With her handkerchief, Miss Vivian dabbed the tears from her eyes and nodded. She reached out and took the bowl that Honovi was now offering her. Honovi left and quickly returned with a portion for Ben and a gourd of water.

Miss Vivian was sure the meal was a mixture of pumpkin, corn, and some type of cooked meat. She was surprised at how delicious it was and ate heartily.

Now that the stress of the trip was receding, both Ben and Miss Vivian realized how tired they were. They scooted their sleeping mats as close to the fire as they dared and stretched out and fell asleep.

Oh'Dar peeked into the shelter to see how they were doing, and when he saw them both sleeping, he retreated and went to find his life-walker.

Instead of sitting at their family fires, Acise, Honovi, and Noshoba were with Ithua at the central village fire. Others were also seated around the circle. Oh'Dar squeezed in and sat next to his life-walker. He put his arm around her and took comfort from her warmth leaning against him, the feel of her inviting body causing him to wonder how they could be alone together.

"How are they doing?" asked Honovi, leaning forward to see around her daughter.

"Sound asleep," he said.

"Try not to worry."

"But I do. I fear I made a mistake bringing my grandparents here. I think they already miss their comfortable life." Oh'Dar ran a hand over his face. "And I picked the worst time. The weather is cold, and even though Kthama is warmer than being directly outside, it will not be the heated environment they are used to."

"Change is always hard. If they had the imagination to come, they will see it through. You said they were bored with their life, and they have not even met your people yet," Honovi smiled with a twinkle in her eye.

Oh'Dar laughed. "Yes, you are right. Now they are exhausted. In the end, what started out as a grand adventure turned into an ordeal. Once they are rested and meet my parents, their passion will flare again."

As they all sat together, Honovi told him about the bonding of Pajackok and Snana and how the couple had just recently returned from the camp Pajackok had built.

A little later, Chief Is'Taqa showed up and sat down on the other side of Honovi. The others nodded at his presence to honor him, as was customary.

Acise leaned into Oh'Dar and whispered in his ear. "I have good news, life-walker. I am with child!" she glowed, pulling aside her winter wraps to show him her tummy.

Oh'Dar's mouth dropped open. "Oh, that is wonderful. How long have you known?"

"I suspected before you left, but I wanted to wait until I was sure."

Oh'Dar pulled her closer to him and hugged her.

Then Acise turned to the others and announced, "I am bearing Oh'Dar's child!"

Many came over to congratulate them, and once things had settled down, Acise said to Oh'Dar, "You must tell your grandparents. It may give them great pleasure."

Oh'Dar felt a sense of calm wash over him. *If I had not gone when I did and had stayed long enough to learn she was having a baby, I would not have been able to leave until after it was born. That would have meant next summer. How could I have stayed away from my grandparents for almost two years, with no way to get word to them? They would have been frantic with worry. Despite my concerns, my timing was right.*

Having slept a while, Ben awoke close to twilight. He looked over at his wife, who was still sleeping. Gingerly rising, he stepped out of the shelter.

A way off was a large fire around which sat many of the villagers. He stood watching for a while. Looking up to see Ben standing there, Oh'Dar rose and went to him.

"Your grandmother's still asleep. It's going to be dark soon; is there any way to light the shelter other than by the firelight?" Ben asked.

"No, I'm afraid there isn't—only the fire. Everything here runs by the rising and setting of the sun. "

"I'm worried that if she wakes in the night and the fire's out, your grandmother won't remember where she is."

"I'll stay with you tonight if you wish, and keep the fire burning," Oh'Dar offered.

"It's your first night home with your wife. I can't ask you to do that, Grayson." Ben had a sudden thought. "While we're here, shouldn't we address you as Oh'Dar?" he asked.

"That would make sense. The Brothers don't know me as Grayson," Oh'Dar grinned.

"Now, return to your wife. I'll know if Vivian awakes," Ben said.

Oh'Dar thanked him and returned to the fire. He knelt down and whispered something in Acise's ear. She got up, and as they scampered away, Acise looked back pleadingly at her mother. Honovi nodded and waved them off. She glanced across at Is'Taqa, remembering the pleasure of their reunions whenever she returned from helping Adia at the High Rocks.

The next morning, after they had eaten, Oh'Dar and Acise entered their shelter together to tell his grandparents their good news.

Instead of Grayson Stone Morgan the Third, Miss Vivian saw Oh'Dar of the People standing before her. She took a moment to assimilate the hide tunic covering his tall frame and the deerskin leggings that led down to fringed foot coverings. He looked appropriate next to Acise, but Miss Vivian struggled for a moment, wondering if Grayson Stone Morgan the Third would ever again appear in her world.

Oh'Dar broke into her reverie, "Grandmother, Ben, we have good news to share. Acise is expecting a baby."

Miss Vivian's face broke into a large smile. She did not know if it was proper to hug Acise but did so anyway. Acise smiled at the embrace, happy that her news had brought such joy.

Then Oh'Dar took them on a tour of the Brothers' village. He showed his grandparents the different shelters and where the group fire was. He explained that many families kept their own fires at night but that many came to the group fire when it was lit.

After a while, Oh'Dar left his grandmother sitting with Ithua and Honovi at the morning fire and took Ben to see the horses and ponies. They stood for a while discussing the stock and how the horses they had brought could improve the Brothers' lines. While they were there, they checked in on Beauty, Storm, and the wagon team. And their thoughts naturally turned to the two they had left with the Webbs.

"Once you and Grandmother are settled and comfortable at Kthama, I'll make a trip back to the Webbs' town. I placed an order and will need to return to pick up the items anyway. Then I can bring back Rebel and Shining Rose. Storm will have to stay here this trip. And by then, you may have thought of something you want me to pick up in town while I'm there," he added. As he was talking, Oh'Dar wondered if there would ever again be any other trips in that direction.

The two men returned to the group fire, little children running alongside them, partly with joy that Oh'Dar had returned but also with curiosity about the older Waschini man.

Honovi and Miss Vivian seemed to be having a pleasant conversation. Oh'Dar listened in while the others around the fire cocked their heads and smiled at the unfamiliar Whitespeak.

Soon the children became bored and ran off, at which point Honovi turned to Oh'Dar. Switching from English, she said, "At their camp, Pajackok and Snana were visited by three Waschini riders. That is why they returned early."

Oh'Dar kept his face neutral. "Was there trouble?"

"There could have been, but Pajackok said one of the Waschini told the others to back down. But they also made some threat about owning the land someday," she added.

Oh'Dar frowned as a worrisome thought crossed his mind. He set it aside and asked, "You are worried that they followed Pajackok and Snana here?" He felt he was being a little rude by leaving his grandparents out of this conversation, but he did not want to disturb or confuse them.

"No, but I do know you are worried about your grandparents being discovered. Miss Vivian told me the story of how you set it up to look as if they had died. I understand the need for the deception—to keep others from looking for them."

"None of us liked the deceit, but we felt it was the only way to end any curiosity about where they went." Oh'Dar sighed. He looked over to see his grandmother watching him with love in her eyes.

He turned back to Honovi. "I need to get them to Kthama. I cannot risk their being discovered here. Even though the riders would not recognize them, word could be carried back that two older Waschini were living in one of the villages." Then he added, "But they have not yet even adjusted to here. How do I introduce them to the People?"

"I would start with your mother," suggested Honovi. "The People's females are not that much different from us, other than in size and strength. It will be easier for them to adjust to Adia than to your father."

Oh'Dar thought about what she was saying. Yes, his mother would seem like a large darker-skinned Waschini. Not nearly as intimidating as Acaraho or the other males. He nodded, his decision made.

Then he turned to his grandparents, "I know you haven't yet settled in, but I want you to meet my mother as soon as you're up to it."

Ben and Miss Vivian glanced at each other. "Why would we not be up to it?" Miss Vivian asked. "Oh. I see—" She remembered him telling them that his people could be intimidating.

"The People are kind," put in Honovi. "They are peace-loving. They want only to live in harmony with the Great Spirit. You have nothing to fear from them."

Just then, Chief Is'Taqa rode in with a group of braves, back from a hunting party. They dismounted and handed their trophies to the women. The group admired the turkeys, grouse, and rabbits.

Miss Vivian tried not to stare at Chief Is'Taqa as he joined his wife at the fire. He was a handsome man and carried himself with authority, yet at the same time, he seemed approachable.

"You are becoming comfortable here?" he asked, nodding at Ben and then looking at Honovi, who immediately translated.

"Yes," Ben said. "We thank you for your hospitality."

"The circle has come around," responded the Chief.

In confusion, Ben looked at Miss Vivian, then back at the Chief, who explained.

"So many years ago, your grandson, Oh'Dar, was abandoned not far from here. The one who found him, Adia, Healer of the People of the High Rocks, first brought him to our village. One of our new mothers nursed him and went with the Healer to help tend him for a few days. Now, you, his family, have also come here. The family circle is completed. It is good."

Miss Vivian hesitated before asking, "Would it be

possible, could we—see where he was found? And the graves in which my son and daughter-in-law were buried."

Chief Is'Taqa looked at his life-walker for her thoughts.

"We understand your wanting to go there," said Honovi. "I suggest we wait for Adia to arrive, and then we can all go together. It was she who rescued Oh'Dar. She should do the re-telling."

They all nodded at the wisdom Honovi had spoken.

Oh'Dar stood up. "I should send a message asking my mother to come as soon as she's able. So, if you'll excuse me—" He got up and walked away.

"Is he going to Kthama now?" Miss Vivian asked Honovi.

"No. Oh'Dar is going to ask one of the People's watchers to carry the message back to Kthama."

Honovi explained about the watchers and how the previous High Protector of the People of the High Rocks had offered to place some within the Brothers' territory to help look for Waschini riders. She explained the little she knew about their roles, how they helped monitor the weather and alerted the hunters to the presence of game, including the migrating herds.

After some time, Oh'Dar rejoined the group, knowing that his mother would come as soon as she was able. How he longed once more to see the love for him in her eyes and feel her protective presence.

The message was delivered to Acaraho, who immediately went to his mate. "Oh'Dar and his grandparents are now at the village. He asks that you come to meet them."

"So, they came, after all! You must come with me," she said, her eyes lit with happiness because her son was back safe and sound.

"He asks that you come alone. He said that in meeting you first, they would have less of an adjustment to make."

Adia nodded thoughtfully. "I will make arrangements for An'Kru and leave as soon as I can."

"I have had a room made ready for them. It is close to the surface, where there will be more light. And I will tell the community that we are expecting unusual guests and remind everyone that it will be a difficult transition. I will also meet with Haan and explain all of this to him."

Adia walked solemnly through the woods to the Brothers' village. Her thoughts returned to when she had first discovered the small Outsider infant. The horrific scene and the moment of indecision where she had struggled with the fearful voices reminded her she would be breaking Sacred Law. The soggy ground gave way under her feet; the sky overhead was a sharp blue. The birds that stayed for winter flitted from limb to limb and sprinkled their song across the silence.

Despite all the beauty surrounding her and her joy at Oh'Dar's safe return, a sadness filled Adia's heart. It was not from her reminiscing; it was something else, but she could not grasp hold of it. She knew it was not unusual for new mothers to go through a dark time after giving birth, and she wanted to dismiss it as that but could not. *Something is waiting to be made known. Something that will be difficult to bear. Great Mother, give me peace to weather whatever it is. I pray for the protection of all those dear to me and all our people, the Brothers, Oh'Dar's Waschini family, and our new friends, the Sarnonn.*

As she approached the edge of the village, she stood a moment, waiting to see where the others were. She could see Oh'Dar and Acise playing with Noshoba while others watched. Her eye quickly caught the figures of Oh'Dar's grandparents, easily spotted with their peculiar clothing and light skin. And the grandmother's hair! Adia had never before seen hair the color of ochre. Even as far away as they were, she sensed their weariness, mixed both with excitement and trepidation. *They are courageous souls, just like Oh'Dar.*

From the tree line, she called out—a sing-song note she had used with Oh'Dar and Nootau all their growing years. It was their secret call, and Oh'Dar immediately picked it up from among the other sounds.

"My mother has arrived! Wait here," he said to the others.

Ben and Miss Vivian turned to watch him go. They waited, not taking their eyes off the spot where he had disappeared into the woods, waiting for him to re-emerge. They both tried to brace themselves, not sure what to expect but not wanting to react in any way which might appear rude or improper.

Oh'Dar trotted over to the wood line and in a moment he had reached his mother and embraced her. Once again, she said a silent thank you to the Great Mother for his safe return.

"Come," he said and led her into the sunlight.

Oh'Dar stepped out with his mother beside him. Miss Vivian's hand went to her mouth, and she stared unabashedly. As the two approached, Miss Vivian could not help herself; her gaze ran over the Healer from head to toe. The long wavy black hair, large brown eyes, skin the color of sweet cream in coffee. She was very tall. Her arms were defined, and the buckskin she wore followed the lines of her body, showing strength built from hard work and service. She moved with the grace of an animal, yet there was nothing fierce or feral about her.

Adia approached with a smile and kind eyes.

When they were close enough, she spoke, and Oh'Dar translated for her, "Blessings. I am Adia, the Healer of the People of the High Rocks. I welcome you on behalf of my people."

Miss Vivian was not sure what to say; she was still blinded by the vibrant beauty of the creature before her.

Ben had instinctively stood up. "Thank you," he said, "thank you for accepting us into your trust."

Adia came over and knelt in front of them. She briefly took Miss Vivian's hand in her own and stroked it, looking down at the gnarled fingers resting in hers. Oh'Dar translated as his mother said, "I know your pain and your joy over your grandson's journey. May the new life that awaits you here bring you much happiness."

Miss Vivian looked into eyes so kind they seemed to soothe her heart at its very depths. She nodded and said thank you.

"My mate, Acaraho, who is the Leader of the People at Kthama, is preparing a living area for you," Adia continued. "We hope it will please you. He is speaking with our people, and they will welcome you. Whenever you are ready, we will be ready for you to join us."

Just then, Honovi and several other women came bearing gourds of hot tea, which Oh'Dar's grandparents took readily, glad for the warmth of the containers. Miss Vivian sipped the beverage and was pleased to find it palatable.

Once they were settled, Miss Vivian asked Oh'Dar to translate.

She turned to Adia, "I have in my heart already thanked you many thousand times for rescuing my grandson and caring for him. I never imagined the day would come when I could thank you in person."

Adia reached out and once again put her hand over Miss Vivian's.

"Before we go to where you live," Miss Vivian asked quietly, "would you take us to where you found Grayson?"

Even though Adia had prepared herself for the request, she still felt a punch in her stomach. "Yes. I will take you there, and I will tell you the story of how I found him." Then she asked, "But are you sure you are up to it so soon after such a long journey? It will be difficult."

Ben looked at Miss Vivian and said, "We're ready. We've been preparing ourselves for this."

Adia rose and waited for the others. She had never taken Oh'Dar there. It would be difficult for everyone, and she prayed for strength to help them and herself through it. "It is a way from here. There is much ground to cover."

Ben glanced at Miss Vivian, who nodded.

"Thank you," said Ben. "We're ready."

Adia looked at Honovi to see if she was coming. At that invitation, Honovi also rose.

They walked together in silence. Each step through the deep ground-cover of the forest was made with almost meditative intention. Miss Vivian was going not only to the place where her grandson had been rescued, but also the place where her son and daughter-in-law were brutally murdered. Ben held her arm through most of the journey, partly to steady her as they walked, but also for emotional support.

As they went down a slight incline, Adia turned to tell them that they were almost at the spot.

She stepped into the clearing and looked around. Tall, dry grasses filled the little meadow. The wagon still stood, though rotted and toppling over, and a flood of emotions hit her. It was in many ways as if she had stepped back in time. The horror of the mutilated bodies, the frantic horses, and the hoof prints traversing the area. The deathly quiet and the stench of blood in the air. It all came rushing back, and she closed her eyes, drawing in a deep breath before trying to breathe it all back out of her soul.

Having buttressed her emotions, Adia moved farther in and turned to face the others. "The ground around the wagon was covered in horse prints." She pointed to the area. In contrast to the decay, wildflowers had grown up around the bed, and some faded delicate heads remained, poking through the eroding wagon wheel spokes.

"There were two horses still tethered to the wagon. I freed them, and they galloped off. Whoever was there had only just left. The prints told me they were Waschini horses, as the Brothers do not put hard hoops on their ponies' hooves." Adia paused.

Miss Vivian spoke up, "Please go on."

"After I freed the horses, I came around the side of the wagon and found your son and his mate. I checked each of them, hoping that their spirits still lived. But they were already gone, so I said a prayer for them. As I was turning to leave, that is when I heard the sound. It was as if an arrow pierced my heart. I knew it was an offspring. My knees shook as I listened for the sound again, and I realized it was coming from the wagon. I found him inside; he had somehow been overlooked. He was nestled down safely among some blankets, and when I lifted him out, he looked up at me with those startling blue eyes, as if all was right with the world. I gathered a few of his things—a blue blanket, a little stuffed toy, and a pouch with a locket in it, and I took him with me back to the Brothers' village. It was Ithua, the Medicine Woman, who helped me with him."

After Honovi had translated what Adia had said, Miss Vivian looked around. Off across the clearing, amid the tall grasses, she could see two wooden crosses poking above the brush. She glanced at Ben and walked over.

Miss Vivian stared at the two graves. Carved into one of the rough-hewn crosses were the initials GSM. She leaned over and gently caressed the carvings. Then she closed her eyes, and tears rolled down her cheeks. *My son. My beloved son. My firstborn. Oh, the hours I rocked you and cared for you, looking into those beautiful blue eyes of yours—my joy at your first steps, your first words, the merry times we had together. How you loved your father and dreamed of taking over Shadow Ridge one day. If only I could see you one last time. Tell you how much I love you. But it's been years since you moved on, unfairly torn from me, whisked away to a place beyond my reach, never to feel my arms again. But I pray that somehow you hear the words of my heart and know I will never stop loving you, and that I have found some peace in being able to stand where you rest.*

Miss Vivian's thoughts turned to her other son, Louis, who was responsible for the graves in front of her. She pushed the thought aside, still unable to bear the loss and betrayal she felt now as acutely as the day Ben had told her of Louis' involvement in the murders of Grayson and Rachel.

Waiting a distance away, the others left Miss Vivian to her grief. When she was ready, she returned to the others. Ben placed an arm around her waist, protectively drawing her to him.

"Some time after," said Honovi, "Waschini riders came to our village. They were looking for the child. They searched our village and found nothing, but they must have found the area where it happened and buried your loved ones. For this, I am grateful," Honovi said.

"When my son and his wife didn't return, we knew something was wrong," said Miss Vivian quietly. "The authorities sent out a search party. They came back and told us they had found this site and buried their bodies. They told us they'd searched your village but decided you were peaceful and none of your people were involved. When they found no sign of—" she stopped a moment and gathered herself. "They told us they couldn't find the baby. It was then they suspected he'd been kidnapped and told us to expect a ransom demand. They posted signs all over the towns between here and there, but there was no word of him."

Ben put his arm around her. "When they couldn't find Grayson's body and determined it may have been a kidnapping, it opened the possibility that he might still be alive somewhere," he said. "I watched Miss Vivian waiting for years for the ransom note. Yet none came. Still, it gave her hope. If it hadn't been for that, I believe losing her family this way would have killed her."

Adia asked, "They caught the men involved, did they not?"

"Yes," said Miss Vivian. "It was only later we learned that Louis, my other son and Oh'Dar's uncle, was involved. He'd hired the men to kill them, all of them. At the trial, one testified that something startled them—someone coming down through the woods—and they panicked. They rode off in a hurry, completely forgetting about the baby."

Adia became very still and quiet. "What is it?" Oh'Dar asked.

Adia closed her eyes and put a hand to her mouth. Thinking.

Finally, she opened her eyes and said, "It must have been me. It was me they heard, coming through the woods. It was my approach that scared them off."

Oh'Dar put his arms around his mother's shoulders. "Then you saved me twice, first by scaring them off and secondly, by rescuing me and raising me as your own. Though you tried to protect me, I have heard stories. I know you paid for that decision at Khon'Tor's hand. I do not know how you could forgive him for the misery he caused you. But you did."

Adia could not help it; tears streamed down her face, and she sobbed for a while. After a long moment, she was able to control herself again and lifted her face to say, "Something compelled me to go that morning. I knew I had to go, even though Khon'-Tor, our Leader at the time, was away. It was an unshakable urging, so I surrendered and gathered the Goldenseal I was to take to Ithua. But the river was up, and I could not cross where I usually would have, so I had to take a longer way around. Otherwise, I would never have come here. The Great Mother, in her wisdom, in her perfect timing, led me to you. Why I was not in time to save your parents, I do not know."

Miss Vivian placed a hand on Adia's arm, and the two exchanged glances. They stood a moment and then turned to look around one last time.

"Thank you for bringing me here," said Miss Vivian, taking another last look at her son's resting place.

Then they reverently and quietly made their way back to the village.

After the evening meal, Adia said she would return to Kthama. She offered to take some of the grandparents' things with her, and they picked through everything to give Adia a basket of items to carry back. Oh'Dar said he would arrange to bring the rest of their belongings later as he could not get the wagon up to Kthama, nor would he want to try for fear of leaving tracks.

It had been an emotionally trying day. At the end of it, having bid Adia farewell, Oh'Dar lay with Acise in her parent's shelter as his grandparents were still in theirs. Honovi and Chief Is'Taqa were still out by the evening fire, purposefully stalling to give the young couple some time alone.

Acise was curled up against Oh'Dar, her head resting on his shoulder. She toyed with a strand of his hair, knowing it would be some time yet before it grew out in the style the braves wore.

"Will you be gone long?" she asked.

"To Kthama? I do not know. Long enough to get them settled. At some point, I need to head back toward Shadow Ridge to pick up supplies I ordered in the town closest to here. Items my grandmother suggested to help with teaching Whitespeak to the offspring and others. And few ideas I had to help make her and Ben comfortable. Why?"

"I missed you, that is all." She raised her face to kiss him.

"I promise you I will hurry. I do not wish to be very far away from you, especially at this time, but I also need to take care of everything ahead of the worst weather, which is about to settle in. Things will soon return to normal. I promise."

Then Oh'Dar turned on his side to face her and gave her what she wanted. Soon, joined as one, they found escape in each other's arms from all that was weighing on their minds.

CHAPTER 5

Acaraho had been busy preparing a room for the grandparents. He selected vacant quarters not far from the main tunnels, yet a little bit out of the flow of traffic. He wanted them to be able to get around easily yet not feel overwhelmed by the daily activity.

Mapiya and her helpers had done their best to make it welcoming. As they had for Adia and Acaraho at the Leader's Quarters, they chalk-washed the walls, and from the ceiling, they hung decorative dried flowers and calming herbs. They picked out the most luminescent fluorite stones they could find and placed them under the sunlight that streamed through the overhead ventilation shafts. An assortment of gourd bowls and cups were brought in. Some of the females had even tried making some flatter forms that Oh'Dar had described one day, to replace the large leaves that the People usually used to serve their food.

An oversized sleeping mat was in a far corner, close to the personal-use area. The females stood in the doorway as Acaraho inspected everything.

"We do hope they will like it," said Mapiya.

"They will, and Oh'Dar will be grateful for your kindness," Acaraho told her.

Just then, a messenger arrived to tell Acaraho that Oh'Dar had asked for help to carry his grandparents' belongings to Kthama. He had also asked that Adia return with the carriers, as hers was a familiar face.

Acaraho turned to the messenger. "Go and alert the High Protector, Awan. Ask him to assemble four of his best guards and meet me in the Great Entrance. I will find my mate and be there momentarily."

Soon, Adia and the males were assembled, and they set off to the Brothers' Village.

The village had awoken, and the Brothers were going about their day. Oh'Dar explained to his grandparents that Adia was on her way back with help to cart their belongings to Kthama.

As they were speaking, there was a rustling from the brush not far away. Miss Vivian and Ben turned to see Adia stepping out from the shadows. She gestured at whoever was behind her, asking them to wait. Oh'Dar went to show his mother where the trunks were that held his grandparents' belongings.

Adia then stepped toward Ben and Miss Vivian, who greeted her warmly. Oh'Dar explained to them that she had brought helpers.

The Healer turned and called out, and those who had come with her slowly came out of the shadows.

Miss Vivian stifled a gasp. "They're huge," she whispered to Ben.

"They're— I don't know what to say," he stumbled. "Giants, really. Very much like us, only so much larger. Well, except for all the fur. Or hair. Or whatever it is."

Oh'Dar directed the males to where the trunks were, explaining that they were fragile and must be carted carefully.

Miss Vivian and Ben waved their goodbyes to the villagers present, checked the shelter for anything they might have left, and prepared to leave with Oh'Dar.

Honovi stepped forward, "May I come with you and stay for a few days? It might help, having another translator."

"That would be wonderful," said Adia. "You know you are welcome any time."

With everything gathered, they made their way to Kthama, frequently stopping to accommodate the slower pace and shorter strides of Oh'Dar and his grandparents.

Though nearly all the leaves had fallen, the profusion of trees was comforting. Sunlight sprinkled down through the tangle of branches overhead. A few forest creatures scampered across the path, and the group traveled in silence, leaving the grandparents to their own thoughts.

As they approached Kthama's Great Entrance, Adia turned to address both Ben and Miss Vivian. "We are almost there. When we enter, you will see only my mate, Acaraho. He has ordered nearly everyone to evacuate the halls and passageways to give you time to adjust to Kthama itself without other people around. Oh'Dar has told me it will be very different from how you have always lived; we do all recognize that this will be a huge adjustment for you."

Ben took his wife's arm and searched her expression, stepping forward only after she nodded; she was ready.

Together they both picked their way up the incline. Years of use had packed it into a hard surface, worn and easily followed. Even so, they barely looked up, so carefully were they watching their footing. Finally, they stopped and saw Adia just inside a large opening, waiting for them to join her.

They stepped inside.

Ben looked across the vast expanse of the Great Entrance, at the smooth worn rock floors, at the walls that rose to a nearly unimaginable height. Stalactites dripped moisture from the ceiling, creating small puddles and rivulets of water along the perimeter. The air was cool with a tinge of humidity that made it feel warmer than outside.

As they were taking in the size of the entrance, a large figure stepped out of a tunnel opening toward the back and off to the left.

Both Ben and Miss Vivian froze, seeing as magnificent a creature as they had ever seen in their lives. From his towering stature, his wavy raven hair, finely chiseled features, broad shoulders, on down to a darkly haired chest, nipped waist, and bulging thighs, neither could take their eyes off of him.

"This is my mate, the Leader of the High Rocks, Acaraho."

Honovi translated, her female voice matched to Adia's.

Acaraho walked over to them, and this time, Oh'Dar translated. "Greetings. You are welcome here."

Ben and Miss Vivian thanked him. Acaraho motioned for them to continue on and down into the corridor where Mapiya was waiting to show them to the quarters that had been prepared.

"Come," said Adia. "I will explain some features on the way to your quarters."

As they walked, Adia talked about the tunnel system connecting the different levels of Kthama and showed them the markings, which they would learn to understand in time. She took them through the Great Chamber, where Mapiya was waiting to tell them about general eating times and so on. Honovi and Oh'Dar took turns translating.

Along the way, Ben remarked, "How is the air so fresh? I'd have expected it to become stale and harder to breathe the farther in we went."

Oh'Dar told them about the Mother Stream, and the Gnoaii where the People kept captured live fish to augment their winter meals.

"Later, I will tell you about the storerooms, water storage, and other things. But for now, we are simply taking you to your quarters," Acaraho said as he indicated a wooden door ahead of them.

The door was constructed of saplings lashed together with vines and leather strappings. Ben looked it over as he and Miss Vivian stepped through the entrance.

Miss Vivian looked around the large quarters. "Much bigger than I'd have thought," she whispered to Ben. "And charming, really." She stepped a few feet further inside, her eyes taking in the light rock walls, the adornments hanging from the ceiling. She spotted the large stuffed mat over toward the back, immediately realizing it was a sleeping area.

"This is beautiful," she gushed. "Thank you so much."

Acaraho nodded and looked across at his mate.

"Honovi will be staying a while to help with communicating," Adia explained, and Mapiya, who had joined them, hastily left to prepare another living space.

A few moments later, the males carrying the luggage came down the hallway. Ben and Miss Vivian stepped aside as the three trunks and the blankets, pillows and other items were brought in and gingerly set down against a far wall.

"Take some time to settle in," said Adia. "We will send someone when it is time for the evening meal. If you are hungry now, there is an assortment of foodstuffs in the work area over there."

"I'll stay with you a little while and explain some of the other features," offered Oh'Dar. "Then you can rest."

Once they were alone, Miss Vivian exclaimed, "I wasn't just being gracious, Grayson. Oh, dear. We should be calling you Oh'Dar, shouldn't we?" she caught herself.

Oh'Dar grinned. "If you wish, yes."

His grandmother continued. "This is beautiful. I can see they went to a lot of trouble to make it comfortable for us. I didn't realize until now how much comfort I take from being inside. I've always enjoyed the outdoors, but it was in the house that I felt the most at ease."

"In time, perhaps this will feel like home, of a type," he answered.

Oh'Dar then explained how the water baskets worked and how the refuse containers were emptied every day but that for now, someone would take care of those. He explained how others would not enter their quarters without invitation and would use the rock on the floor just outside the door to draw attention to their presence.

Miss Vivian was listening but could not wait any longer and went over to the trunks, lifting the lids, trying to find the one with her personal belongings in it. She pawed around a bit until she found her favorite teacup, so carefully wrapped by Oh'Dar. Letting out a long breath, she smiled widely when she discovered it had survived unscathed.

She carefully put it back before running her hands over the inner rock wall.

"Not as cold as I'd have thought," she murmured. Then she walked into the private area, came back out, and announced, "I just figured out what that room is for!" and they all laughed.

Oh'Dar watched her as she continued around the room, running her hands over the large rock slab that served as the work counter and food preparation area, noting the boulders and wood stumps placed for seating. She peeked into the lidded gourds and baskets, learning that some held water, some held dried meat, and others held nuts. She looked up at the hanging baskets overhead.

"What a beautiful pattern. From the size of the People's hands, I wouldn't have thought they could produce such a tight weave," she commented.

Oh'Dar replied, "I wove those at first. Then I taught the youngest possible offspring, with the smallest hands, to do the same. They hold your daily water supply. Those in here are smaller than the others use, because water is surprisingly heavy. The smaller baskets on that counter hold enough for a day's supply. Anyone would be glad to help you refill them if you need help with the hanging baskets."

Ben's eyes never left his wife as she explored their new home.

"There's a great deal to learn," said Oh'Dar. "Tonight, in the Great Chamber, you'll be among many of the People. That's where most of our social events take place. I suggest you both get some rest as this has probably taken more of a toll on you than you realize," he cautioned.

Miss Vivian nodded, and Oh'Dar left them to make themselves at home. As he was leaving, his mother was coming back down the passage.

"I wanted to give them this in case they are cold." She held up a large wolf hide. "I know Kthama often feels cold to you when the rest of us are still comfortable."

Oh'Dar hugged his mother and stepped aside to let her pass.

She called out before entering.

"I meant to bring this earlier but forgot. Here, in case you need it." As Oh'Dar translated, Adia draped the beautiful fur covering over one of the seating stones.

"Wait, please," said Miss Vivian as Oh'Dar continued to translate. "Before you go, I must thank you again for saving my grandson. And for raising him. He's a fine young gentleman, and I owe that to you. How can I ever thank you?"

"I cannot imagine what you have been through," said Adia. "All those years. Praying that your grandson was still alive but having no real hope that he was. Yes. I went through trials to protect and raise him. There were many nights I cried, pleaded for wisdom, prayed I would be able to help him make a life for himself here. But, despite my efforts, he would never physically be one of us, and there was a hole in his spirit that longed to find a place with others of his kind, where he might better fit in."

Adia paused a moment, "When he left to look for you, it took all my strength to find the faith that he would return to us someday. And then, when he did, the burden of who he was had been lifted, only to be replaced with a new one. And that was his anguish over longing to be in two worlds. When he was here, he worried about you. When he was with you, I have no doubt he worried about his family here. Now you are with us, and his heart is finding its peace. So the only thanks I could want from you is that you find your way to be happy here. Though we cannot fully comprehend what has changed for you, everyone respects that you have made a huge commitment in giving up your elder years of comfort and familiarity for the love of Oh'Dar. And for that, I owe you a huge debt of gratitude."

Tears in her eyes, Miss Vivian reached out and took one of Adia's hands. Separated in experience by two different worlds, but joined at the heart by the same love for Oh'Dar, and both united in their commitment to do all they could to help him find peace, the two smiled at each other.

❦

Once they were truly alone, Miss Vivian exclaimed, "Oh my. They're all magnificent. So healthy, so vibrant. So alive and filled with—something. I'm exhausted and excited at the same time."

Ben sat down on the sleeping mat. "Come here, my dear." He reached for her. "I can see how excited you are, but I also know that Grayson is right; you really do need to rest. We both do."

Miss Vivian reluctantly calmed down and went and sat next to her husband. She let out a huge sigh, "Yes, now I do see how tired I am. You're right; we need to rest." And she lay down next to him. Both she and Ben were asleep within moments.

❦

Pakuna came to collect them when it was time for the evening meal. She could not introduce herself, so she had stopped first to collect Honovi.

Oh'Dar's grandparents were ready and waiting, though Miss Vivian was fidgeting on her seat and jumped when they clacked the announcement stone.

Honovi introduced Pakuna. "She will be coming

to get you if I am not here. She will also be working with others to help you maintain your quarters, such as bringing you water, disposing of waste, and other tasks. Pakuna was one of those who cared for your grandson directly. She was his wet nurse."

I hadn't imagined anything like this, marveled Miss Vivian. *Nor thought about all those who banded together to help raise and protect Grayson. I'm anxious to get back here tonight to talk to Ben. He's probably seeing even more details than I am.*

"Pakuna is taking you early, so the Great Chamber will be mostly empty," Honovi said. "Everything has been planned as best as possible to ease your transition. Before you came, their Leader, Acaraho, met with the entire community and told them about you. Of course, everyone wants you to feel at home, though they have as much curiosity about you as I am sure you have for them."

In her nervousness and excitement, Miss Vivian had not considered that, though in hearing it, she was ashamed of herself for being so self-absorbed. *This is a big change for us all.*

Ben observed closely as they made their way to the eating area. He was counting the steps and turns, eager to be independent as soon as possible. They walked into the Great Hall and saw the rows and rows of rock slab tables, seating benches, and individual seating boulders. He looked around at the huge cavern, empty except for a small group of three and some females who were watching them enter from behind a counter.

Pakuna led them over to the females. Along the counter's surface, various fruit and nuts and dried meats were spread out with large leaves stacked in between. Pakuna gestured for them to select what they wanted. When they hesitated, Honovi went ahead and helped herself before turning for them to do the same.

Ben looked around, noticing there was no water anywhere. Guessing at what he wanted, Pakuna picked up a gourd from a nearby table and handed it to him.

When they were finished, they followed Pakuna over to a seating area near the back.

With Honovi translating, Pakuna explained, "Families have their usual tables. The Leader and his family sit over there. If you are comfortable at the back here, this can be your place. On other occasions, it would not be unexpected that you sit with the Healer Adia at the Leaders' table, as Oh'Dar is her son."

They all sat, and Ben and Miss Vivian hungrily ate everything they had selected. Seeing their servings gone, Mapiya brought them some more. They looked up to thank her, and she smiled, revealing her sharp canines.

At that moment, the reality of their situation came crashing in on Miss Vivian, and she started to cry. Just then, Oh'Dar entered, and seeing his grandmother in tears, came running over. He slipped in next to her and pulled her into his arms. "Grandmother, what's wrong? Why are you crying?" He looked at Ben for help.

"I don't know son, everything was fine until a second ago."

"A second ago," Miss Vivian murmured, still in Oh'Dar's embrace. "A second ago. What does that mean? It doesn't mean anything any longer. I don't even know what time it is. What day it is. Where's my clock?" She pulled her head from his embrace, "Grayson, Ben, where is the clock? I don't know what time it is!"

Seeing that she was becoming hysterical, Oh'Dar put his hands on her shoulders and turned her to look at him.

"Grandmother. Look at me. This has been too long a trip, and it's too much of a shock; I see that. I know you've been brave and put up a strong front, but you're only now realizing just how much everything has changed for you and Ben."

She nodded through her tears, trying to find her handkerchief to wipe her eyes.

Wanting to help, Pakuna handed her a piece of hide of the kind that they used as cleaning cloths. Miss Vivian took the foreign object, looked at it, and started crying harder.

Just then, the offspring of the other family sitting there came slowly walking over. She stood quietly to the side, waiting for Miss Vivian to notice. When she did, the little female said, "You are the Miss Vivian. Please, the Miss Vivian, do not make tears. Do not be afraid. We are here to love and help to you. We wait for you with eager wanting."

Miss Vivian's crying eased, and she stared at the little female who stood in front of her. Dark tangled hair framed her face, and the deep brown eyes were filled with kindness. Her little hands remained at her side, yet she was leaning toward Miss Vivian just enough to signal that she wanted very much to hug the Waschini woman.

"She— She—" Miss Vivian looked at Oh'Dar.

"The school, remember?" he answered. "There are quite a few of our offspring who will be able to talk to you and are anxious to meet you."

She looked at the little female, who glanced back at her parents. The mother nodded, and the offspring took a step forward with her arms out, offering a hug.

Miss Vivian opened her arms in an embrace and rested her head against the offspring's hair, which smelled of pine and sage.

"What's your name?" Miss Vivian asked, releasing her from the embrace.

"Nasha," the offspring answered.

"I'm happy to meet you, Nasha."

"There is hope in me to much talk with you," said Nasha.

"The sentence structure is different," explained Oh'Dar, "but she's making great progress."

Scampering back to her mother's embrace, Nasha's face lit up with a huge smile as she told her parents what she had said.

Ben moved closer to Miss Vivian and asked her if she was alright now. She nodded, smiled, and apologized to Mapiya and Honovi.

Adia and Acaraho had walked in at the end of the drama and stood waiting for it to conclude.

Adia said to Acaraho, "I thought they needed several days' rest. Now I am wondering if perhaps what they really need is to find some purpose here. Perhaps tomorrow, Oh'Dar should introduce Miss Vivian to his students. Just for part of the day. And for Ben, a tour of the rest of Kthama and perhaps a conversation about the Wall of Records."

"It is too soon to take him to Kht'shWea; they are not ready to meet the Sarnonn," Acaraho answered.

"No, I agree. But perhaps the thought of it will occupy Ben's mind and help him start feeling he can contribute."

"You are right. Oh'Dar could never compete with his peers on any physical level, and as an adult, he is still not able to make the same contribution to the community as the other males. It is just like that for Oh'Dar's grandparents. Each of us needs a place from which we can give of ourselves."

When Miss Vivian's smile returned, they approached the group and greeted each of them.

"In the future," said Acaraho, "You will be welcome at our table—once you are more accustomed to the activity here and ready to join us at the regular mealtime."

Then Adia addressed Oh'Dar. "Please may we speak with you?" After excusing themselves, the three of them stepped away.

Acaraho explained what he and Adia had just discussed.

Oh'Dar expressed his agreement with their plan before adding, "I have not had a moment alone with you. So much happened on the way here, but most urgently, I must tell you there is another community of Sarnonn living in the area of Shadow Ridge."

Acaraho frowned hard, "What?"

"Yes. It is such a long story, and it involves the Mothoc Guardian, Pan."

Adia said, "We must hear this. Alone somewhere." With Handspeak, she explained to Honovi that they needed to leave for a while. Honovi signed back that she would take care of Ben and Miss Vivian until they returned. The couple watched them signaling back and forth to each other and waited patiently for Honovi's explanation.

In one of the chambers that had long ago been turned into a meeting room, Oh'Dar relayed what had happened at Shadow Ridge and how he had met Notar at the Masons' farm. He told them Notar's story about Pan coming twice to their community. Then, and once decades previously. He told them that Notar's appearance was the event that had sparked Mrs. Mason to make the stuffed toy that was with Oh'Dar when Adia rescued him.

When he was done speaking, both Adia and Acaraho remained silent for a moment.

Acaraho spoke first. "Haan must be told. Do you have any idea how large Notar's group is?"

Oh'Dar shook his head. "Nor would he tell me how to make contact again."

"Still, the fact that another Sarnonn community exists provides hope. As soon as possible, Oh'Dar, I need you to come with me to Kht'shWea to tell Haan this."

"Of course. But first, tomorrow I will take my grandmother to meet the school children. I agree that we need to get them both established and engaged in something."

※

The next morning, Oh'Dar took Miss Vivian to the schoolroom. Mapiya had spread the word that school would be reconvening that day. Oh'Dar stood with

Miss Vivian as they watched the offspring file in and take their seats.

"The children don't look that much different," she said. "Just larger than their true age, I imagine?"

"Yes. The clothing some of the offspring wear makes them look foreign to you, but if they were dressed in Waschini—dressed as we—" Oh'Dar struggled to find the words.

"Yes," she said and patted his arm.

When all had taken their places, Oh'Dar introduced his grandmother to the offspring.

"We are glad to the meet make of you Miss the Miss Vivian," said one of the smaller females from the front row.

Others echoed her sentiment. At the back was little Nasha, the female who had come to comfort Miss Vivian the night before.

Miss Vivian smiled at her and gave a little wave, though she did not know if it was a gesture they used.

"Miss Vivian is going to be working with you, too. Perhaps not every time, but often. This morning we are going to learn different names for common items we use."

Oh'Dar showed his grandmother where to sit and then went to the front wall, which had been fitted with slate. He picked up a rough piece of chalk and started to draw trees, animals, baskets, flowers. He named them in the People's language, then named them in Whitespeak. As she watched and listened,

Miss Vivian repeated some of the words as best she could, trying to learn for herself.

When they had finished for the morning, many of the offspring came up to speak to her directly. Tears welled in her eyes and threatened to slip down her cheeks. *This is just what I needed. Grayson is so smart. I see now that Ben and I will be left out of the general conversation less and less as more of them learn our language—and as we learn theirs.*

After the offspring had left, she inspected the chalk drawings.

"Could I learn to speak their—your—language?" she asked.

"I don't know why not," said Oh'Dar. "But it might be helpful to start with learning Handspeak. That's how Honovi taught me as a child, combining Handspeak with English."

"What do I call the language they speak?" she asked.

Oh'Dar pondered for a moment. "How about Akassan?" he suggested. "That's what the People are called by the Sarnonn. The Akassa."

"Akassa," she repeated. "And that Sarnonn fellow we met—when will we meet the others?"

Oh'Dar laughed, "I thought you might need some time before you met them."

"Well," she laughed, "I probably do. But I'm not so sure about Ben. I think he's raring to jump into all of this."

"I'll let my father know—" Oh'Dar stopped, embarrassed.

Miss Vivian put her arm around him. "You don't have to worry about offending me, Grayson," she explained. "I know that in every way that matters, Adia is your mother, and Acaraho is your father. Let's speak freely with each other and not worry about saying something insensitive. I know you love Ben and me, and I also know that these people here are your family, too. More so than we are. It does not hurt our feelings to acknowledge that."

Oh'Dar hugged his grandmother. "I'll have to leave before too long. I need to travel back to pick up some supplies I ordered at Wilde Edge. Paper, quills, ink, and some other items. I won't go until you're comfortable here without me, but I do need to go before the truly harsh weather sets in."

"Maybe you can ask one of your most advanced students to help us translate?" she asked.

"Honovi will have to return to the village at some point, so yes, that's a good idea; I'll give it some thought."

As they finished their conversation, Mapiya came to tell Oh'Dar that his father was waiting to speak to Haan. Oh'Dar asked her to find someone to show Miss Vivian back to her quarters and went to find his father.

Acaraho was in the Great Entrance, along with his Circle of Counsel.

Haan had just arrived. He had assembled his own Circle of Counsel, and together they all went to a meeting room.

Haan introduced each of his group; his mate, Haaka, as Third Rank, Artadel, the Healer, as Second Rank, High Protector Qirrik, and Sastak, who represented the females. He had also included both Lellaach and Thord, the paired Leaders of the Sarnonn Guardians.

Acaraho did the same; introducing Adia, Healer and Second Rank, Mapiya, the spokesperson for the females, High Protector Awan, Nadiwani, Oh'Dar, and Thetis, whom Awan had selected to be First Guard.

Oh'Dar recognized Thetis as the guard who had gone with Acaraho the first time they used Kweeuu to track Tehya and rescue her from Akar'Tor. He had also been present when Khon'Tor nearly killed himself with the Waschini knife.

All eyes were on Oh'Dar as he told the story of meeting Notar and what the Sarnonn had said about Pan's messages.

"How are we to find them," Haaka pondered aloud.

"I suspect that when the time is right, they will find us," said Haan. "If the Guardian Pan has ordered Notar's steps through the decades, there is no reason to doubt she will manage to let him find us at the appointed time."

Adia spoke next. "Pan is to train the Sarnonn Guardians as well as An'Kru. Yet has anyone seen her walking Etera?"

"We have met with her," said Thord. "But not on Etera. You know the place, Healer, it is what you call the Corridor."

All eyes turned to Adia. "The Corridor is another reality. It is a place that both Urilla Wuti and I have visited many times. It is from these visits that we bring back the information we share." She turned to Thord, "Is she training you there?"

"For now," replied Lellaach. "Later, our training will take place on Etera."

Before changing the subject, Acaraho glanced at his mate to be sure she was finished. "Haan, as I said might happen, Oh'Dar's Waschini grandparents have come to Kthama. His grandmother will be helping teach White-speak to our offspring. His grandfather has an understanding of bloodlines, and we will be asking him to work with the researchers once he is comfortable here."

"If he does not know our language," asked Artadel, "how can he help with bloodline research?"

Oh'Dar looked at his father for permission to answer. "He will learn it in time. But until then, he can look for patterns. The markings are symbols, after all. I believe he will be able to help."

Oh'Dar went on further to let them know of the

Waschini riders who had accosted Pajackok and Snana and made some threat about taking the land.

Acaraho ended the meeting by saying that he would be sending a message to the People's Overseer asking to address the next High Council meeting to relay this same information to them.

When they returned to Kthama, Oh'Dar and his parents went to find Ben and Miss Vivian. They were with Honovi in the Healer's Quarters.

Both grandparents looked up as the three entered.

Honovi said, "I am teaching them some Hand-speak. They are quick students."

Acaraho asked Honovi to translate for him. "When you are ready, Ben, we will ask for your help in trying to navigate the challenges of our bloodlines. It will be some time before you can discuss this with our researchers, as you will need to learn our language to do so. But we look forward to any help you can give us before then."

Having been through the Great Chamber earlier and noticed more people there, Ben said, "It seems that your women outnumber your men?"

"Yes," Acaraho said as Honovi continued to translate, "At present, that is true. A contagion came through some time ago, and we lost many of our males. So our need is even more urgent. Our researchers have reported that if we do not find a way to introduce new bloodlines, we will become extinct in seven generations."

"Extinct?" Ben looked at Oh'Dar.

"To the point that breeding will produce deformities and handicaps. So rather than do that to the offspring, the People will choose instead to die out."

Ben thought for a moment, "Why are the Brothers not experiencing this?"

Honovi explained, "We are a small community, but our people do not usually take partners from our village. It does sometimes happen, as with my daughter Snana, but we have many more communities and far greater numbers than the People do. We meet with other villages and find partners—in that way, we do much as the People have done for centuries through the Ashwea Awhidi."

"The Ashwea Awhidi is the People's pairing ceremony," Adia explained. "When someone of age asks to be paired, the researchers check the bloodlines to find a good match. Occasionally, a couple from the same community will fall in love. That pairing also has to be blessed by the researchers before it can take place. However, it does not happen too often, as our offspring are taught about the importance of pairing outside of their own community."

Ben nodded. "You're all a great help to us, thank you," he said to Honovi.

This time, Oh'Dar translated as Adia said,

"Acaraho and I must travel before too long to another community to attend a High Council meeting."

Oh'Dar sighed. "And I need to return to Wilde Edge to pick up some things. I don't want to leave, but I'm concerned about the harsh weather that's about to begin in earnest."

"I can stay at Kthama for a little while, Oh'Dar, if you must leave now," Honovi said, "but I must return home before too long."

"You should go soon," said Adia. "The weather will be turning harsh."

Miss Vivian spoke up, "Please go. Please don't cause yourself travel problems. We'll be fine here. Even if Honovi has to return to the village, Nasha can communicate with us fairly well. We'll get by."

"It will be a while before I can get back," Oh'Dar said. "And as you know, you can only very rarely return to the village—it's just not wise. We took care to stage your deaths so people wouldn't ask after you, and with the Waschini riders coming through, you could be spotted and cause questions to be raised."

"We understand, son," Ben said. "We'll be fine. Truly."

CHAPTER 6

It was some time since Newell Storis had received the letter from young Mr. Morgan asking him to intervene with the bank in Wilde Edge that was threatening foreclosure on Matthew Webb's homestead. He knew enough of the story to understand Mr. Morgan's connection with these people and had no problem writing to the bank and taking care of the Webbs' debt. But something lingered, which he couldn't shake.

Despite the Sheriff's assurance that everything about the death of the young man's grandparents was on the level, he couldn't get out of his mind how they'd died.

He looked around his office at the dwindling stack of work to be done. The town wasn't the same without Miss Vivian. Shadow Ridge went on under the ownership of Mrs. Ermadine Thomas, who was content simply to keep the place going and wasn't involved in business dealings as the Morgans had been. Storis had since been there several times to finish up some final paperwork but always refused to look in the direction of the stables where Miss Vivian and her husband were killed by Rebel. Rebel, who still hadn't been found, even though posters were put up and the usual gossip had carried the story far and wide. A horse like that was virtually priceless.

Storis' last visit had been so depressing that he now vowed never to return unless absolutely necessary.

It was the first Grayson Stone Morgan who had given Storis his start by taking the young lawyer under his wing. Over the years, the Morgans became the primary client of his business. When Mr. Morgan senior passed, Miss Vivian had ensured that Storis kept their business, so losing the connection with the Morgans was a blow as much emotionally as financially.

He turned down the gas light that was illuminating the office and casting shadows on the walls. Everything reflected his mood. Somber, grey, empty.

He locked the front door behind him and made his way to the room he rented over one of the local Millgrove establishments. Alone in the world, with no wife or children, and having lost his connection with Miss Vivian, he saw nothing ahead for him but the eventual decline of his business.

I need a change of scenery. I need to get out of this town for a while, clear my head.

By the time he'd closed the door of his room behind him and hung up his coat and hat, he knew what he was going to do.

⁂

Mrs. Webb and Grace were putting the bread in the oven when they heard a knock at the door.

"Who could that be?" Mrs. Webb asked aloud as she wiped her hands on a cotton towel and brushed off the front of her smock.

Grace followed as her mother went to the door and opened it. Outside stood a decent-looking man with strong features, dressed in big city finery. Mrs. Webb's eyes dropped to the large leather bag he was holding at his side.

"Are you Mrs. Matthew Webb?" he asked?

"Why, yes. What can I do for you?"

"My name is Newell Storis. I was Miss Vivian's—Mrs. Jenkins'—lawyer, and I was hired by young Mr. Morgan to take care of some business with the Wilde Edge bank."

Mrs. Webb looked at Grace, "Please go and find your father."

Grace headed for the door, and Storis apologized and stepped out of the way.

"Come in, please." Mrs. Webb led the lawyer into the sitting room and showed him to the best chair.

A few moments later, Grace returned with her father.

"I'm Matthew Webb," he said as he held his hand out to Storis. "What's this about? My daughter tells me you're the Morgans' lawyer."

Storis leaned over and opened the brown leather case he'd brought with him. He pulled out some papers for Mr. Webb and snapped the top shut.

"These are the papers showing that your mortgage with the Wilde Edge Bank has been settled. Grayson Morgan the Third, Mrs. Jenkins' grandson, instructed me to take care of this for you. You'll have no more trouble with it. He also had me set up a trust to provide for your welfare. The papers explaining how it works are with the others."

"That's very generous," answered Mr. Webb. "We have fallen on tough times since I had my accident."

"There's also provision to compensate a local family to continue helping you with your farm work. Should that fall apart for some reason, you're to contact me, and we'll make other arrangements," he explained.

"I see; thank you," said Mr. Webb. "And where is your business?"

"Up until recently, I'd have said in Millgrove. That's the town nearest Shadow Ridge. But now that Mrs. Jenkins and her new husband are gone, I find myself at a bit of a loss as to how to continue."

"Well, we'd be glad if you would stay for supper," Mrs. Webb told the lawyer. "And if you don't have other arrangements, you're welcome to overnight here as well,"

Newell Storis took a moment and looked intently at the family members gathered around him. "I appreciate the thought."

"While you think about the offer, let's show you what Grayson and Ben did for us," Mr. Webb put in. "We also have a son, who helped out a great deal, but he's not here at the moment. He wants to become an animal doctor, and he's out on rounds with our current one."

"Now that we have help around here, he can spare some time to go after that dream," added Mrs. Webb as they left the house.

Grace tugged on one of the barn doors, and slowly it swung open. The warm scent of hay and animals wafted out from inside.

Watching where he stepped, Storis entered. He immediately spotted them. "These look like Morgan horses."

"They are," responded Mr. Webb. "Grayson left them with us. He couldn't immediately take them, but I imagine he'll be back before long."

Storis looked over the stunning beasts. "Definitely Morgan stock, such superior horses. It was terrible about the accident."

"Oh, I know," Mrs. Webb said. "I didn't realize you knew about that. I imagine Grayson wrote you somehow? Yes, we were anxious for a while that Miss Vivian might not recover."

Storis' head snapped around. "Miss Vivian? You

mean Mrs. Jenkins?" he asked carefully, and his eyes darted about as if looking for a stronghold.

"Yes. Miss Vivian is what she told us to call her," she answered. "And we were told to call her husband Ben. She said it was too formal to address them as Mr. and Mrs. Jenkins. I meant no disrespect."

"I— I didn't realize you knew them."

"We knew Miss Vivian from when she first came to get Grayson," explained Mrs. Webb. "But we hadn't met her new husband, Ben. As you said, there was the accident she had crossing the river. We truly were afraid she'd die of pneumonia. Though Grayson and Ben got her here as quickly as possible, she was still chilled to the bone."

Storis dared not move lest he betray his inner turmoil. "And this was when?" he asked in a measured voice, his brows in a hard knot.

"They left a bit under a month ago," she said. "I'm sorry, Mr. Storis. I thought you knew about this. I guess Grayson didn't want to worry you, so he didn't mention it."

"Perhaps if you start at the beginning?" he suggested.

"There isn't much to tell," she said. "Grayson and his grandparents—he calls them that even though we know Ben isn't a relation—were on their way through. Crossing the river, the horses spooked. Miss Vivian was standing up in the front seat of the wagon because she was worried about Grayson. He'd jumped into the water to lead the team across. Then the current shifted the wagon, and she fell overboard. Grayson rescued her, but she was drenched and caught a chill. Our Dr. Miller brought her back to health, and they went on their way. But Grayson didn't want to fool around with the two extra horses, so he left Rebel and Shining Rose here and said he'd be back."

"Rebel?" Storis nearly choked.

"Yes, why?" she asked. Storis could feel Mrs. Webb scrutinizing him, searching his face for something.

"Oh, nothing, nothing. I see," he said. "I'm sorry; I must be tired from the trip. If you don't mind, I'd like to take you up on the offer of staying here. It's very kindly of you."

"You're welcome," smiled Mrs. Webb. "Come on, let's get you inside. Do you have bags with you?"

"Yes, but only one."

It was decided that Ned would immediately go into town with Mr. Storis to help the lawyer bring back his things.

✿

At supper, Storis was still reeling from the shock of learning that Miss Vivian and Ben were still alive.

Once everything had been passed around, and plates were full, Mrs. Webb asked him, "Do you have a large practice back at Millgrove?"

"Not since the—since Mrs. Jenkins—Miss Vivian

—and Mr. Jenkins left town. They were my primary clients." He changed the subject. "This sure is some good home-cooking. I don't get much of that."

"Are you not married? Do you not have a family?" Grace asked.

Mrs. Webb frowned at Grace for asking such a personal question of someone they didn't know. Storis saw the look pass from mother to daughter and said, "It's not a problem, Mrs. Webb. No, Grace, I don't. I suppose that's why I feel the loss of Miss Vivian so greatly. She and her first husband did a lot for me. Helped me get established. In a way, they were like family," the lawyer explained.

"That must have been hard for you then—their deciding to leave," Mrs. Webb said.

"Yes. Very much so," he answered.

He next addressed Mr. Webb. "You said young Mr. Morgan would be back for the horses. Have you any idea when?"

"No, but I suspect before too long due to the weather turning. And Grayson said he ordered some supplies that he'll need to pick up at the General Store before heading back."

"I have some business I'd like to look into tomorrow," Storis said after a moment. "I may be gone all day."

"Certainly. You'll be back for supper?" asked Mrs. Webb.

"Yes, thank you, I will," he replied gratefully.

That night as they lay together in bed, Mrs. Webb said to her husband, "What a decent fellow. But he seems disturbed in a way I can't quite put my finger on. I imagine he's just distraught over Grayson's grandparents leaving Shadow Ridge. It's a shame he's all alone in the world, isn't it?"

"Now, Nora. Don't be getting any ideas about Grace and that lawyer man. He's much older than her. And you don't want her moving away, now do you?"

His wife sighed. "I suppose. But there isn't anyone here she's interested in. And it's not unusual for a grown man to wed a younger girl. She is of age. And she'd be well taken care of; I don't want her to struggle if I can help it."

"I think you're getting ahead of yourself. Mr. Storis isn't staying, and there isn't time for anything to grow between them. Let's go to sleep, and you can get that notion out of your head." Mr. Webb rolled over and turned out the light.

Like many small towns, there was the customary local establishment where men gathered to trade, gossip, and drink. Storis stood in the doorway and glanced around. Several men sat at the bar while others were sitting at the scattered tables. As he entered, he noted a tall man in tattered clothing leaning against the wall to the left of the door. Storis crossed the roughhewn floor to the bar.

The bartender called out, "What will ya' have?"

"Whiskey."

The bartender brought it promptly. "You're not from around here. What's your business?"

"I'm just passing through, but I'm considering bringing my business here," Storis said and threw back the shot.

"Guessing by how you're dressed, you're a banker?"

"Lawyer," Storis responded.

"As long as you're not up to making trouble, you'll find yourself welcome here."

"There's something you could help me with," Storis said, taking a coin out and placing it on the table.

The bartender looked down, and his eyes widened. "What do you want?" he asked.

"I'm looking to hire a tracker. Know any?"

The bartender glanced over Storis' shoulder. "Might. What're you looking to hunt? Bear? Cougar?"

"Not hunting. Tracking. And it's not an animal; it's a man." He glanced back to see what had the barkeeper's attention.

The tall, rugged fellow pushed off from the wall and sauntered over to the bar. He leaned down and looked Storis in the eye.

"A drink for my friend here," said the lawyer,

meeting the man's gaze and laying another coin on the bar.

※

After a few days, Storis announced to the Webbs that he'd be returning to Millgrove but that he might be back someday as he was considering moving his business to Wilde Edge.

"Is that what you were doing in town?" asked Mr. Webb.

"Part of it. I met with the banker there, and he assured me they could use a local lawyer. Surprised me, given the size of the town, but apparently, with all the homesteading going on, there's a need. It seems a lot of land out here is unclaimed."

"Odd to think our little town might grow, but I guess that's what they call progress," said Mrs. Webb.

"I did check with the bank, and all the arrangements that young Mr. Morgan put in place are holding up. I'll be leaving today, and I thank you for your hospitality. May I avail myself of it one last time and get a ride to town later today? There's a carriage heading back that leaves at five o'clock, and I'd like to catch it."

"Of course. I'll take you myself," said Mr. Webb.

"May I go too?" asked Grace.

"Yes, you may come this time," said Mr. Webb, giving his wife a look as if to say again, *don't get any ideas.*

On the way into town, Grace politely asked Mr. Storis what it was like to be a lawyer. They chatted good-naturedly, and from what Mr. Webb could tell, Mr. Storis didn't seem to mind.

I wonder if Nora is right. They do seem to get along. And if he is moving his business here— Well, I won't rule it out altogether. But I'm not going to encourage it either. The last thing I want is for Grace to get hurt. He's far more sophisticated than any of us around here. Though Grace would make anyone a fine wife. She's as smart as a whip, a great cook like her mother, and very good-natured.

CHAPTER 7

Accompanied by Harak'Sar's males, Khon'Tor trudged through the damp leaves, headed out on what they all believed to be an impossible task. Still, they were committed to giving it their best. A lost offspring was a heartbreak no one should endure. Several had families of their own and understood that if there was any chance at all of finding the young one, they had to take it.

As they talked together in silence, Khon'Tor's thoughts returned to Tehya, and he wondered what she was doing in his absence. He knew she was being cared for, but he longed to return home to the comfort of her arms. *Home. Will the Far High Hills ever feel like home? Will the longing to return to Kthama ever cease?*

. . .

Khon'Tor, so seldom separated from Kthama by any distance, had been practicing what his father taught him about the energy lines that flowed throughout Etera. The lines the sentries and watchers used to navigate. Lines that would lead him to distant communities of the People. He had let this ability lapse, having had no need of it as, for the most part, he only accessed the communities further up the Mother Stream. He knew his sensitivities were nowhere as strong as those of the watchers, but he felt as if they were now on a fairly direct line toward the Far Flats. When the group stopped for a rest, Khon'Tor asked, "Am I correct that the current feels as if it is broadening?"

"Yes, it is indeed less focused here and a little more dispersed, but it still leads to the west," said the lead watcher.

Khon'Tor ran his hand through the silver white streak in his crown and was silent a moment. "I feel we would be wise to split up a bit, perhaps a watcher and two guards together. The first three sweeping slightly north, the other three keeping to this, the main path, and I will follow the lines further to the south."

"Will you be able to find your way?" the watcher asked.

"Yes, I believe I will. I have been working on my long-neglected abilities to feel the currents. We all know that without preparation, Berak would not have survived much farther than this. And we are about at the limit of our supplies; if we are to make it back ourselves, we need to turn around within the next few days. I suggest that we continue in these differing directions, and if we do not find any sign of him in that timeframe, each group should independently head back."

The watchers and guards nodded and headed off as instructed.

The cold air chilled his lungs, and he wrapped his cloak around him more snugly. His feet were protected from the newly frozen ground, twigs, and stones, and on such a long journey, he was glad for the foot coverings. There was no path where he was heading. Along the way, he kept his senses peeled for any sign of unusual activity. A broken tree limb, trampled leaves hinting at a sleeping area. Each time he paused, he ran his hand up and down through the crown of his hair. Then he set out again.

At nightfall, Khon'Tor looked for a small overhang to provide protection from the elements. Gathering mosses and leaves, he made a place to sleep and covered himself with fronds and fir branches. He turned his thoughts to Tehya, warm and snug in their quarters under the wolf pelts they had brought from Kthama. He comforted himself by thinking of Arismae tucked safe and cozy into her little nest. Khon'Tor did not know how long he would be gone but was committed to continuing until his heart was satisfied that he had done what he could to find the offspring.

Every so often, he paused and searched his gut feelings for where he should go. At night, he checked the constellations, keeping his direction consistent. Though he was in unfamiliar territory, he knew if he traveled far enough along the magnetic lines, he could easily retrace his steps.

Maybe being stripped of everything that defined me will teach me how to recreate myself. Open me up to a different way of being. All my life, I have been a Leader. Perhaps now it is time to learn to be a follower—to follow something other than my own reason, will, feelings. To tune into the wisdom the Great Spirit gives to those who ask. It is true that I am no longer who I was; perhaps this is helping me figure out who the krell I am supposed to be now.

He pushed himself each day, along the way gathering what he could of roots and foliage, supplementing it with a ration of dried meat from his satchel.

Time passed until Khon'Tor's supplies reached breaking point and he knew he would have to turn back the next morning. Then, almost at nightfall, he detected a nauseating stench not far ahead. He decided to continue and find the source.

Before long, he was standing over the rotting corpse of what had been one of the People. It could only be Berak; of this, Khon'Tor was suddenly certain.

So, you were headed to the Far Flats, after all, he thought as he looked down at the decomposing mess. *But where is the offspring? My son. Another son I can never claim.*

Khon'Tor searched the area but could find no sign of the offspring. There was nothing—not a torn piece of hide, a discarded cloth, a tiny body. All he could do was to turn back.

Having for days pushed himself to exhaustion, he dropped to his knees and leaned forward and doubled over in anguish, his head in his hands. *You cannot even give me this peace? I do not care that Berak is dead. Better for everyone, but where is the offspring? Though it would not absolve me of my crime against the maiden, if I could at least return the offspring to them alive, it would be some small atonement.*

He finally straightened up and ran his hand over his crown as was his habit. A strange feeling washed over him, and he became very still. *The offspring is alive; I can feel it. But where?*

After Khon'Tor had taken care of what was left of Berak, he turned and started the long trek back to the Far High Hills, his heart heavy with the knowledge that he had not found any sign of the offspring. It was clear that at the time of Berak's death, U'Kail had not been with him. Along the way, he called out in case the others could hear him, but knowing that in time, if they had not already, they would also trace their way back.

Word had reached Tehya that Khon'Tor was close to the Far High Hills, and she was impatient for his arrival. Estimating his time of return, she had left Arismae with her parents so she would be free at any time to go and welcome him.

Finally, Hollia, Urilla Wuti's Helper, came to find her, excited. "He is almost here. Come! Urilla Wuti is also on her way!"

The Helper did her best to keep up with Tehya, who sprinted through the passageways to be there when he walked in.

Harak'Sar was already waiting, and Urilla Wuti and Iella showed up shortly.

Before too long, Khon'Tor's silhouette appeared in the entrance and Tehya ran to him.

"You are back. Oh, Adoeete," she cried and buried her face in his chest."

"Saraste', please, I am in great need of cleaning up," he said, though kissing the top of his mate's head.

"I do not care. You are back, safe and sound," Tehya exclaimed and stepped back to look at him.

The color drained from her face. Khon'Tor's foot coverings were practically in shreds and his tunic was grubby and tattered. His beard had grown far longer than he ever kept it, and his hair was greatly in need of care. He had also lost weight.

"Let me tend to you please," she asked, pulling him by his hand to lead him away.

"In a moment. I must first report to Harak'Sar what I found."

Harak'Sar and High Protector Dreth both stepped forward.

"I found what I am confident was Berak's body," Khon'Tor explained. "He had been dead for some time; I gave him as fair a Good Journey as I could. There was no sign of the offspring, nor any sign that it was with him when he passed."

Harak'Sar nodded slowly. "The watchers have reported that three other males are also on their way back."

"I split us up to cover more ground, so a second group should also be reporting back soon."

Harak'Sar shook his head. "It is my hope that your effort will at least provide some peace to Larara and Linoi's parents."

Khon'Tor nodded slowly. He turned as he saw movement, and out of the corner of his eye, he could see that Nootau had joined the group and was studying him.

Urilla Wuti stepped forward to face Khon'Tor.

"The offspring is still alive; I can feel it," he said, looking steadily at her.

"I agree with you. Your heart is troubled but rest in the knowledge that you accomplished what you were meant to. Let us pray the offspring will be found at the right time," she offered.

Khon'Tor nodded, and with Harak'Sar's leave, he

left with Tehya, looking forward to the comfort of her love and care.

⁂

Chief Kotori and Second Chief Tawa had asked for Myrica to join them. She stooped down, moving the flap to enter the shelter.

Chief Kotori addressed her. "Ahanu is growing. Already he is stronger than the young children his age."

"He has a joyful gentleness of spirit and he is no threat to them," she answered, eyes downcast. "He is a joy; he is no burden."

"Do not let your heart hide from you the truth of what you know will eventually be. You must be prepared, Myrica. The day will come when he has to be returned to his people," said Second Chief Tawa.

"But today is not the day," she replied.

The two Chiefs nodded.

Outside, Tiponi was waiting for her with Ahanu on her hip. The child reached for Myrica when she re-emerged—the only mother he knew.

"He is heavy," she laughed as she took him from Tiponi, tussling his full head of dark wavy hair, so different from their straight locks.

"And he gets heavier every day, it seems." Tiponi smiled at her friend.

"Chief Tawa reminded me that one day he must

be returned to his people. But when and how I cannot know," Myrica said and sighed heavily.

"Trust that the Great Spirit, who brought Ahanu into your care, will know when the time is right and will make a way to return him safely to his kind."

"But today is not that day," Myrica repeated.

✿

After the other males had returned with no report of any sign of the offspring, Khon'Tor set out to give Larara the news. She and Linoi's parents sat quietly while he relayed his story to them.

Larara spoke when he had finished. "We are grateful for your efforts," she sighed. "I will let my mate know. Again, I apologize that he doesn't wish to meet with you. I have no explanation."

Khon'Tor stood up to go and meet with Berak's parents. "In my heart, I believe the offspring lives. I would not tell you this if I did not believe it to be true. The Overseer, Urilla Wuti, agrees. Let us pray to the Great Spirit that in time he will be returned to you."

"The Overseer," said Larara. "Urilla Wuti is the new Overseer?"

"Yes," Khon'Tor replied.

"I wondered who they would appoint. I am relieved that my mate stepped down. It was too much for him, and during the past year, it seemed to be wearing on him more and more. He hardly seems the person I know him to be."

Stepped down? thought Khon'Tor. *So that is what he told her. I suppose that without saying he was removed, it is the only plausible explanation for why he is no longer Overseer. At least I now know he has not broken his agreement with Acaraho and the High Council by speaking of what really happened. Between that and how she has been treating me, Larara does not suspect I was the one who took her niece Without Her Consent.*

On his way back to the Far High Hills, Khon'Tor once again had time to think. *Despite my efforts to avoid deception, it follows me. But what of this offspring? It is a male, so what if it favors me as did Akar'Tor. Must I live the rest of my days with my sins hanging over my head? The wounds on my back are healing, but the scars on my soul may never heal. Perhaps only when death comes will I find true peace.*

Larara carried the news to her mate, Kurak'Kahn, who met her with a stony glare. She had hoped for his comfort, that together they might find solace.

"Have you nothing to say?" she finally asked him.

"What would you have me say?" he asked, his voice flat. "I am happy to hear that Berak is dead, I will say that. But what is it you want to hear from me? Do you want me to say how thankful I am that Khon'Tor took some of his precious time to look for

U'Kail? Well, so what. He did not find the offspring, did he? So we are no further ahead than we were."

Larara shook her head. "I no longer know who you are. This bitterness you feel toward Khon'Tor—whatever it is you are not telling me, please, I beg of you, tell me now," she pleaded.

"If I told you the truth, it would only drive this wedge further between us. So if you are going to leave me, do so quickly," her mate said sourly. "I have nothing to tell you; nothing that can change what has happened."

Larara stood and looked at Kurak'Kahn for a while.

"Are you speaking of Bak'tah-Awhidi?" Her voice broke.

If I tell her that Khon'Tor raped Linoi, she will ask how I know. And Acaraho was right; I cannot prove it. But she will not let it go; she will push and push and push for an answer. Eventually, she will go to the High Council and ask one of them about it, and then Acaraho will know I broke the agreement. And he will tell her the truth, that I tried to murder Khon'Tor; that I dishonored my station as Overseer. And I will be banished for breaking my word. At that point, I will lose her anyway.

Kurak'Kahn finally looked at his mate. "It is no use. There is nothing for us to share together except more anguish and suffering. You are better off without me. You can stay here, with what is left of our family. Ask for Bak'tah-Awhidi; I can virtually guarantee you that the High Council will grant it.

Then perhaps, alone, we can each salvage something of what is left of our days here on Etera."

Silence.

"Larara, send a messenger to the Far High Hills and ask when the High Council will next be meeting. When you find out, let me know. I will go there with my belongings to ask for a place in another community."

Larara stared at Kurak'Kahn for a while, but he did not meet her gaze. Then she turned and went to find a messenger.

Oh'Dar had been traveling for some time. He hated to have left his grandparents and Acise but knew he had been right to go. Winter had descended and it would be a race to get to Wilde Edge and back before the heavy snowfalls hit.

He urged the team on, grateful that the Webb's little town would soon come into sight. He was looking forward to seeing the Webb family again. Though the trip had been long, especially traveling alone, he had spent a great deal of the time in prayer to the Great Spirit. He had not only asked for guidance but had also given thanks for the blessings in his life. However, he was anxious to return to be assured that both Acise and their offspring were doing well.

Grace ran out of the house when she heard the wagon approach. "Mama! It's Grayson. He's come back!"

Before long, Mrs. Webb came out of the house. "How good to see you," she said. "You're back sooner than we expected."

"While you were gone, the lawyer came with the papers from the bank!" Grace said.

Oh'Dar's face blanched. "He came here? Mr. Storis?"

"Yes," said Mrs. Webb. "He brought the papers himself. I'm not sure why; perhaps he didn't trust them to get to us otherwise."

Oh'Dar's mind started whirring. He didn't want to ask too much and raise suspicions by the nature of his questions.

"How long are you staying?" Grace asked.

"Only a few days. The items I ordered are ready, so tomorrow I'll return to town and load them up, then set out early the following morning."

Snide Tucker stood in the tavern looking absent-mindedly out of the window at the general store across the street. He had a coin in his hand and was tossing it up and catching it again. *So Storis was right. The man sure wasn't hard to miss. And the storekeeper told me he'll be coming back tomorrow to get the materials he ordered. Best I'm ready to leave by then,* he thought.

With everything loaded on the wagon and secure, Oh'Dar returned to the Webbs for the rest of the day. As he'd said he would, he rose early the next morning, and with a basket of food Mrs. Webb had prepared for him, started out on the journey back to the Brothers' village. *I still don't know why Mr. Storis would come to Wilde Edge. Even if he has heard about my grandparents, I've no intention of returning here for a very long time, and he has no way of finding me.*

Far enough behind not to be discovered, the best tracker known for hundreds of miles around was following Oh'Dar's trail.

Back at the Far High Hills, Iella continued to hone her new ability to communicate with Etera's creatures. She used her free time to practice reaching out to them. She was relieved to learn that they were voluntarily communicating with her and that she was not compelling them to do as she asked. In no way did she want to have dominion over them.

She sat perched on a moss-covered rock and eyed

the bobcat that stared at her from the fallen trunk of an old Oak tree.

The bobcat stood perfectly still, eyes locked on hers. Iella dropped into the center of her soul and bade him sit. And he sat. Then she asked him to stand up and walk the length of the trunk. He did as she asked.

"Thank you, brother," she said aloud. "Be on your way now until we meet again." *This is truly remarkable. I do not know what to think. I have no idea why I now have the ability or what I am to use it for. But I am sure in time the reason will be shown to me. Thank you, Great Mother; may I learn how best to serve you with this gift you have granted me.*

⁂

Urilla Wuti left word for Khon'Tor to see her. He found her in the Healer's Quarters with Nootau. Standing in the doorway a moment, he watched them before he announced himself. *How do the People not see me in him?*

"You asked for me?" he finally said.

Urilla Wuti turned to him. "Thank you for coming. Please, sit." She indicated one of the seating boulders.

Khon'Tor wanted to remain standing, but out of respect for the Healer, he sat.

"Harak'Sar has come to me with his concerns about the offspring of Adia and Acaraho," she said.

"He told me he has also shared those concerns with you."

He nodded slowly and waited for her to continue.

"I believe Haan's proclamation about An'Kru. Everything in me resonates with that truth. But I also agree with Harak'Sar's wisdom, that whatever peace may be coming will not necessarily be easily ushered in."

Khon'Tor remained seated, watching her.

"Nootau, here," she said, motioning to the young male. "We have been told that he will play an important role with An'Kru. We are not sure what that role will be, so we must be open to any possibility."

Khon'Tor did not ask from where Urilla Wuti got this information. He accepted it as more of the Healers' world to which he was not privy.

"But where there is light, there is also darkness," she added. "It is possible that there are—elements— that do not wish to see this come to pass."

Finally, Khon'Tor spoke. "You fear Adia's new offspring may be in danger?"

"Harak'Sar considers it a possibility," she answered. "As do I." She walked across and sat down next to Khon'Tor. "Here, you are too far removed," she said. "You must leave your family and return to Kthama."

Khon'Tor could not suppress the frown that heavily creased his brow. "Kthama?" His heart seemed to sink and leap at the same time. "To what purpose?" he asked. "What do you expect me to uncover? A plot among the People of the High Rocks to harm the offspring?" he scoffed, not catching his reaction in time.

Then he paused and sighed. "I apologize, Healer. Overseer. I do not mean to be disrespectful, but if I were to return, what of Tehya? Arismae? And I am to start training Brondin, Harak'Sar's oldest offspring. Was anything spoken of those?"

"We are not suggesting you move there permanently. But much is changing and whatever happens will start there. That is where the primary vortex is, and everything points to Kthama being at the center of it all. We cannot wait for news to reach us here. By then, it may be too late."

"I must speak with Tehya about this. And with all due respect, Harak'Sar himself."

"Perfectly understandable," spoke a voice from the doorway. Everyone turned as Harak'Sar walked in.

"While you were out looking for Berak and any sign of the offspring, I spent a great deal of time in meditation and reflection," said the Leader. "I was seeking wisdom from the Great Spirit, and my gut feeling only grows stronger with each day. Now I believe you need to be at Kthama, and I believe Nootau must go with you."

"What of Acaraho," said Khon'Tor. "He has barely established his position."

"You are concerned your presence will usurp his authority. I understand that. This is why I suggest you move into Kthama Minor with Haan and his people. That way, you can interact with Kthama but not be there every moment. And now you are wondering if Acaraho, Adia, and Haan will be in accord with this. I believe that other leaders have felt whatever currents are moving outside of our awareness to prepare us for what is to come. I assure you that they will also recognize the need for your presence. However, I will send a messenger to Adik'Tar Acaraho and let him know you are coming at my request, and why."

"And Nootau?" Khon'Tor asked, letting himself look at the other son he could never acknowledge.

"I agree with Harak'Sar," Urilla Wuti stated. "Nootau must go with you."

"I can be ready to leave whenever you are," Nootau said to Khon'Tor. "Iella already knows of this and understands."

"Very well. If it is permissible, I would like a few days before I leave Tehya again," said Khon'Tor.

"Of course," said Harak'Sar.

"When you go, please carry a request to Acaraho," said Urilla Wuti. "Ask him if we may once again use Kthama as the location for the High Council meetings. Now that we are including the wider circle of Leaders, Kthama is the only location that can accommodate such numbers. If he agrees, ask him to send messengers to the other communities to tell them of the change in location. And ask if I may have a private area, separate from the High Council meetings, in which to meet with the Healers and Helpers."

"I will carry your requests, Overseer," Khon'Tor answered.

He returned to find Tehya seated on the floor of their quarters playing with Arismae. The offspring had some of Tehya's wrappings and covered her head with them before peering out at her mother and giggling.

Tehya turned as Khon'Tor greeted her. He sat down with his family and picked up Arismae, holding her close. She reached up, grabbed hold of his beard, and hung on tightly. As she tugged on it, he chuckled and looked down into her golden eyes. "Arismae, you look like your mother more and more every day," he said to her.

Then he hiked her further up, onto his shoulder, and carefully hugged her tighter.

"Saraste', I do not want to tell you this, but Harak'Sar has asked me to go to Kthama and stay there for a while."

Her eyes got wide, "Without us?" she asked.

"Yes. It has to do with the offspring, An'Kru," he answered.

She closed her eyes tightly. "So soon. So soon," she said quietly. "You just got back."

"I do not have to leave for a few days," he answered.

Tehya rose to her knees and reached for Arismae. "Before you leave, we will make the best of your time." She leaned forward and pressed her lips tightly against his.

With Arismae tucked into her nest, Tehya led Khon'Tor to their sleeping mat, and they spent the rest of the afternoon in each other's arms. It was too long since Khon'Tor had enjoyed his tiny mate and he took his time with her, claiming her again and again until both were exhausted and fully satisfied.

CHAPTER 8

In silence, Khon'Tor and Nootau traveled along the Mother Stream. Khon'Tor had never taken a specific interest in Nootau, even though the young male was his son. But now, he found himself curious about who this person had become.

"How is your life progressing at the Far High Hills?" he asked as they walked.

"I am happy to be paired with Iella. And I am grateful to Acaraho for helping raise me," he answered.

Khon'Tor frowned at the choice of words.

"I miss living at Kthama. I hate leaving Iella, but I will be glad to see my mother and Acaraho."

They continued a while in silence punctuated only by the Mother Stream coursing along on the left, carrying life-giving oxygen and nutrients on her way to Kthama and Kht'shWea.

Suddenly, Nootau stopped and dropped his

carrying bag to the ground. Khon'Tor took another few steps before turning back to face Nootau.

"Are you not going to ask me why I am speaking of Acaraho in that way? Are you not at all curious about why I do not call him my *father*?"

Khon'Tor kept his eyes on the young male.

"I know the truth, Khon'Tor. I know that I am of your seed. I know that you took my mother Without Her Consent. And I know that out of the greatness of her heart, to protect our people, she kept your secret all those years—and keeps it still."

Khon'Tor slowed his breathing. For one of the first times in his life, he did not know what to say.

"Despite what you did to her. Despite the years you made her life as hard as possible. Despite her humiliation over everyone thinking she had failed in her calling as a Healer. And even though you let Acaraho take the fall for your doing. Despite all that, she spared your life," Nootau said.

He continued, "And I imagine that the only reason my real father, Acaraho, did not kill you for what you did was that my mother made him promise not to. So she served you doubly."

"Everything you have said is true. Your mother had no fault in any of this. She has treated me with far greater mercy than I ever deserved. You have every right to hate me."

"Do you not want to know how I know all this?" Nootau stared at Khon'Tor as he spoke. "No, my mother did not tell me, though I am sure she wanted to, for many reasons. But instead, she protected you for the sake of the community. For all the communities, because for them to know what you did would have torn our people apart. She wanted me never to know, I am sure, for fear I would think I carried your corruption in my own blood."

Khon'Tor stood still, letting Nootau empty his soul's pain.

"Before my mother's offspring, An'Kru, was born, the Guardian Pan came to me. Since that time, she has come to me several times. During those visits, Pan told me many things, only a small part of which I shared with my parents and most of which I have never shared with anyone. And the truth about who sired me was one of the things she told me. As she instructed, I have mentioned it to no one. It has been hard to hold this, but that is nothing in comparison to the burden my mother has carried all these years."

A thousand questions ran through Khon'Tor's mind, none of which he asked.

"What is coming is going to be harder than anything we have been through before," continued Nootau, "and somehow, you are a pivotal piece of it. Just as she told me I would have a role in protecting An'Kru, Pan also told me that I will protect you. I do not know any more than that. But she said I had to know the truth about you so I could do what I needed to with a pure heart. Before everything comes to a head, I had to know what you did and find a way to forgive you for it."

Khon'Tor finally spoke. "The fact that I am standing here unharmed suggests that perhaps you have."

"I am not there yet, though I am working on it," Nootau said. "My mother shared with me much of her wisdom as I was growing up. One of the things she told me was that forgiveness is not born of a singular point in time. Forgiveness ebbs and flows, and just when you think you have grasped it, it can slide out of reach. It must be won again and again. And each time, it is not an easy victory. But until you reach forgiveness, the wrongdoing that was inflicted holds power over you. Only by genuinely forgiving you will I be freed of the burden of the injustice you inflicted on my mother. Only by forgiving you will I be able to reclaim that part of me that is still imprisoned in the pain of the past.

"Pan also said that once I had confronted you, I must tell my mother and Acaraho that I know the truth of who I am. So they can lose the burden of lying to me all these years because it wears so deeply on my mother's heart and on her soul. She has paid in so many ways for your crimes."

Khon'Tor spoke. "The People still recognize you as 'Tor. You have a right to the leadership of the High Rocks."

"I am still seeking my place, it is true. But I do not covet the role of Leader. If my will could be done, it would never pass to me," Nootau said.

"Because you do not wish to lead." *How different he is from Akar'Tor.*

"Because I wish for Acaraho to live forever."

Nootau's words hit Khon'Tor hard. *The love of a son for his father; one of the greatest blessings in life. Will I ever know that?*

"Is there more?" Khon'Tor asked, thinking of Nootau's twin sister, Nimida.

"Not that I will share with you," Nootau said.

"For what it is worth, I am deeply sorry." Khon'Tor unwaveringly looked Nootau in the eyes.

Nootau turned away and then turned back. "I am not Akar'Tor. I am not blinded by hate for you, Khon'Tor. I have heard the multitude of stories about how you have changed, and I have seen it myself. I see your love for Tehya and your daughter. I grew up on the stories of your great wisdom—stories of your valor and sacrifice. Though we have had little contact through the years, you have done me no direct wrong. So the grudge I bear you is, in a way, not yours to bear. Because I do believe that you are no longer the monster who committed such travesties."

"I have no right to say this, but if I did, I would say I am proud of who you have become."

Nootau answered solemnly. "Perhaps someday that will mean something to me." Then he picked up his bag and slung it over his shoulder before walking away in the direction of Kthama.

Khon'Tor waited a moment before starting after him. *In a way, I feel great relief. These last years, I have in some way wanted him to know. And though I still cannot claim him publicly, there is some peace in realizing that at last, he knows the truth.*

Acaraho, Mapiya, Adia, and Nadiwani were taking a break in the Great Chamber when a guard informed them that Khon'Tor and Nootau had arrived.

Acaraho and Adia exchanged glances and excused themselves to meet the arrivals.

Adia stepped forward to embrace her son while Acaraho greeted Khon'Tor.

"I was told you were coming," Acaraho said. "And as I mentioned before, you are welcome at the High Rocks."

"We are here at the direction of Urilla Wuti in her role of Overseer, and with Harak'Sar's blessing," emphasized Khon'Tor. "They feel it is important for both Nootau and me to be here; they are expecting events to play out in which Nootau and I will have a crucial role. I have no more information than that."

"I was told, and I am in accord with that decision," said Acaraho.

Adia released her son and looked at him. *There is something different about Nootau. He suddenly seems so much more mature, as if he has somehow stepped into a place of certainty.* "What of Iella and Tehya?" she asked.

"They were not told to come," answered Nootau.

"And we do not know how long we are to stay and when we will return home. It is as much a mystery to us as I am sure it is to you."

Adia closed her eyes for a moment. *It feels right that they are here.* And something *has also shifted in Khon'Tor; he is more at peace.*

"You must both come and have something to eat while I have a space prepared for you for tonight, Khon'Tor," said Acaraho. "Nootau has his own quarters waiting for him."

As they walked, Khon'Tor relayed Urilla Wuti's requests to Acaraho.

"I have no problem with that," said the Leader. "I will send messengers out tomorrow with the news of the change of location, and I will gladly arrange a separate meeting room for Urilla Wuti and the Healer network."

Behind them, Adia and Nootau were chatting. "You suddenly seem so grown up," Adia said. "Apparently, being paired suits you."

Nootau grinned across at his mother. "I miss life at Kthama, though. Despite wishing that Iella could be with me, I am glad to be here. And I need to speak with you when we can be in private."

"Of course. After you have eaten, if you wish, we can meet in the Healer's Quarters."

Nootau looked around the familiar room at the dried herbs hanging overhead, the rows and rows of tightly-woven baskets, the lidded-gourds housing the various powders, dried leaves, and roots. He was suddenly aware of the powerful healing energy of the Healer's Quarters.

"So much has changed, Mama," he said. "For one, I can feel the positive energy here. And then, there is Iella; I have to tell you about Iella." He was too excited to know where to start. But over the rest of the afternoon, he told Adia about Iella's sudden ability to communicate with animals, his conversation with Harak'Sar and Urilla Wuti about his need to come here—and more. In turn, Adia told him about Oh'Dar's grandparents, their blossoming roles at Etera, and everything else she could remember that he might not know.

"The coming High Council meeting is very important," she said. "We need to tell the members about the existence of the other Sarnonn community that Oh'Dar discovered during his last visit to Shadow Ridge. And then there is Urilla Wuti's request for the Healers and Helpers to meet separately. Will you be included, son? Have you determined if you are a Healer?" she asked.

"I do not know if I am a Healer proper. There have been certain events, just as I told you about the visit from Pan when she told me about An'Kru and how I would play a role in his life. And I get other messages. Flashes of insight or actual words appearing in my head. Hearing, but not exactly like hearing."

Adia nodded, completely understanding what her son was telling her.

"Mama, I have to tell you something else that happened." He paused. Adia leaned in and quietly waited for him to continue.

"Once, when I was lying down after a hard day's work, I was brought into that place where I first met Pan. The Corridor. Only in this case, I did not meet Pan. I met—" He paused again. "You are not going to believe me."

"I will. I promise," Adia said.

"I met An'Kru. Only he was grown. And he was magnificent. I cannot tell you how drawn I was to him. I did not want to leave his presence."

Adia reached out and squeezed Nootau's hand, "I believe you. Go on."

"He told me to live my life with Iella and not to worry about my role of protecting him—that it would unfold in time. Afterward, I told Urilla Wuti about it."

Adia squelched a pang of jealousy at hearing he had first told Urilla Wuti about his visit with An'Kru. *But he is grown now. His circle has expanded, and he mostly lives at the Far High Hills. I cannot expect him to wait to speak with her until he has confided in me. Great Spirit, give me the strength to release him to walk his own path.*

Nootau continued, "It was then that she decided

the Healers and Helpers must start meeting separately. She believes that many of the Healers may be experiencing something similar to what Iella and I have, all brought about by the opening of Kthama Minor. And maybe amplified by An'Kru's birth."

Adia then explained how she and Urilla Wuti were starting to believe that meeting in the Corridor would allow the Healers to communicate across the far distances that separated them. Nootau listened carefully.

After she was done explaining, she said quietly, "You have changed. It is as if you have come into your own sense of self. Of who you are."

Nootau took a deep breath.

"I know who I am, Mama," he said. "And I mean that in every way."

Pause.

"I know that Acaraho is not my blood father." He had finally said it.

Adia inhaled sharply.

"I know it is Khon'Tor who seeded me. And I know the circumstances."

Adia had to look away for a moment.

"I also know why you protected him all these years and why you had to lie to me to do so."

Tears welled in Adia's eyes.

Nootau reached out and touched her arm. "Do not cry, Mama; I am not angry." And he repeated what he had told Khon'Tor, about how Pan had told him the truth of this and why.

"At the first opportunity, I will meet with Father and tell him," he added. "But as this is so personal to us, I wanted to talk to each of you alone."

"So many times I wanted to tell you. It has been a knife in my heart, not being honest with you. I am so sorry," she wept, "I am so sorry. I pray you can forgive me."

Nootau put his arms around her. "Mama, I love you so much. I know that you were caught in a terrible predicament with no good solution. I know you must have agonized over this more than I can ever imagine. It was a shock to hear it, but I am glad I now know. I am just so sorry this terrible thing was done to you and how you have suffered because of it."

"There is more," she sobbed, thinking of Nimida.

"I know. Pan told me. And she told me you would say that. But she said to tell you that when the time is right, the rest will be revealed and that for now, I know enough. So, please, whatever you were about to say, do not. I am learning to trust the Order of Functions."

Adia wiped away the tears running down her face and turned her head to meet her son's eyes.

She placed one hand against the side of his face, "You are no longer the little offspring who played at my feet. You are no longer the young male who learned at his father's side to throw spears and fish in the shallows of the Great River. You have grown not only beyond my grasp but also beyond my ability to protect you from the harsh realities of Etera."

"I have grown beyond your grasp, it is true. But I will never stop reaching back for it. You will always be my hero, my inspiration. And my Mama."

Adia let herself melt into her son's arms, and she sobbed out the years of pain and anguish in his comforting embrace. They stayed there for some time, healing together, each gaining strength from the other's love, preparing to face the storm that was coming. But at last, the lie that had lived between them since Nootau was born was released into the light of truth.

CHAPTER 9

Oh'Dar was relieved when once again the treetops near the Brothers' village came into view. Dusty and weary from the trip, he paused to change out of his Waschini clothes. He pulled off the hated boots, tipped them over, and shook off the dirt and grime before stuffing them into the bottom of one of the boxes on the back of the wagon. It was too late to pull into the village; he would wake everyone. So instead, he unhitched the team and attended to each horse. He scavenged around and was lucky enough to find enough dry wood for a warming fire. His thoughts drifted to the supplies he had brought, and he hoped he would not have to return to the Waschini world again any time soon.

The next morning, Oh'Dar drove into the village and was met with the usual fanfare of happy children running around and the circle of welcoming adults.

He jumped off the wagon bench, and immediately Acise was in his arms. She smiled and threw her arms around his neck. Then he greeted Acise's family and all the others who were watching intensely. After speaking with them for a moment, Ithua suggested that they all give Oh'Dar and Acise some privacy. Everyone disappeared except Noshoba.

"What did you bring?" Acise asked excitedly.

"Hopefully, things that will make my grandparents' transition easier. I did bring some sweets for the children if you want to get help and pass them out. Oh, and—" He dug around in a bag at the back of the wagon, and finding what he wanted, pulled it out.

She peeked into the open bag and exclaimed, "What in—?"

Oh'Dar laughed and took out something shiny. He put the harmonica to his mouth, bent over to hide what he was doing, and gave it a whispery toot. Acise's eyes widened and she laughed.

"I got them for the children before I left Shadow Ridge. But now that Waschini riders have been in the area, I do not think it is a good idea."

Acise nodded. "Perhaps not."

Oh'Dar put the harmonica back into its packaging, which he wrapped closed. He dropped it back into the wagon.

"I am so happy to be home," he exclaimed, and

picking her up carefully, he briefly swung her around.

"You do not have to tell me that you are anxious to go to Kthama and see your grandparents. Would you like me to go with you this time?" Acise asked.

"I would love that," he said.

She walked around to the back of the wagon and peered in. "Do we get to see what all of this is?"

"When it is unloaded, yes. I am going to need help getting it to Kthama."

"The watchers will help you. They can easily carry everything. It would be much better than trying to get the whole team and wagon up there," she said. Then she noticed her little brother still watching them.

"Noshoba, go and find Momma, please. Oh'Dar and I need to talk"

Oh'Dar tousled the boy's hair before sending him on his way. "He is excited I am back."

"So am I," said Acise, smiling up at him.

He pulled her up close and pressed her tightly against him. "I cannot wait for tonight," he whispered into her ear.

"What is wrong with going to our shelter right now? Or have you become shy while you were away?"

"Nothing is wrong, but I have to take care of the horses and the supplies in the wagon," he answered.

"That is going to take a while," she said.

"All the more reason for you to come with me to

Kthama. By tonight, everything will be taken care of, and you and I can have each other all to ourselves."

"Can the wagon not wait until tomorrow? It will be too late by the time all that work is done."

"Alright. I will take care of the horses now and the wagon tomorrow."

Before she left him to it, Acise gave him a long, lingering kiss.

As Oh'Dar was leading the team away, a figure emerged behind him. He turned to see Pajackok jogging to catch up, with Noshoba not too far behind.

Oh'Dar stopped and waited for them.

As he waited, his mind flooded with bittersweet memories of times together with Pajackok as they were growing up. He had looked on Pajackok as a friend, and he grieved the loss.

"I, too, am glad you have returned to our people," said Pajackok. "If you will allow it, Noshoba and I can take care of the horses. Your life-walker is waiting for you."

"Thank you," said Oh'Dar and stopped to stare while Pajackok and Noshoba continued on with the team. *I believe that was his way of saying I am no longer his enemy.*

As he was thinking, Isskel came trotting over.

"Chief Is'Taqa sent me. One of the hunting parties is back. They saw tracks behind yours, and he wanted you to know that it seems you were followed here."

"What kind of tracks?" Oh'Dar asked, his mind spinning. *Did Notar follow me here somehow? If he did, it is not likely that he would leave any type of track.*

"A Waschini rider; they said there is no doubt about it. The hoofprints stopped at the far ridge. From there, hidden in the firs, whoever it was could easily have seen you come into the village."

"Are there signs they are still in the area?"

"No," said Isskel. "There are return tracks, but we lost the trail after a short distance."

Oh'Dar's stomach knotted. *Who? Who could have followed me? And why? Louis? No, it could not have been Louis. The Sheriff said Louis was going to where he would never be able to escape. An accomplice? Someone he hired? I understand what Isskel is saying, but just because the tracks went back the way they came doesn't mean they are not coming back. Maybe with others.*

"Thank you." Oh'Dar turned and headed for the Chief's shelter.

Acise saw him approaching the center of the village and hurried over. "What is wrong?"

"Change of plans. I need to unload this wagon now. I will talk to the watchers and see what help I can get on short notice. Isskel has told me there were Waschini tracks following me here."

Oh'Dar jogged off into the woods. In the distance, Acise could hear the guttural language the People used to communicate between themselves. The tension in her partner's voice was impossible to miss.

She ran to tell her father that Oh'Dar was going

to bring watchers into the village to help move the wagon. Within moments, Is'Taqa had ordered the village cleared and all the children tucked safely into their shelters with their parents. Little heads popped out to watch as two of the People followed Oh'Dar out of the woods. The two males walked to the front of the wagon and pulled it out of sight into the brush.

A third watcher had hurried back to Kthama to ask for additional help. High Protector Awan rounded up five guards and sent them running to the Brothers' village to help Oh'Dar.

Soon, the collection of males started carrying items from the wagon back up and into Kthama. Before long, the wagon was emptied and the supplies were piled up in the Great Entrance.

Acaraho walked over to ask Awan what was happening.

The High Protector explained and added, "We will leave everything here until Oh'Dar tells us exactly where to put everything.

"Please, on my behalf, thank those who helped."

Awan nodded and surveyed the pile of items clustered together on the rock floor. "Interesting," he said to no one in particular.

Oh'Dar regarded the empty wagon. *I hate to do this, but it has to be done. There is no pretending that this is anything but a Waschini wagon.*

He explained what he needed the watchers to do next.

Once again, the males went around the front of the wagon and pulled. Oh'Dar led them around the village and down a fair length of the path. Acise and Noshoba were following behind.

Finally, they arrived at their destination.

Oh'Dar explained what he wanted, and the watchers set about gathering the largest rocks they could carry and loading them into the wagon bed. Finally, when the wagon was as heavy as it could be without breaking the axles, the watchers regarded Oh'Dar.

After a few more instructions, the watchers pulled the wagon out into the lake as far as they could bear, their curled lips and frowns attesting to their hatred of water.

Then they waded around to the back and pushed with all their might. With the water seeping around it, the wagon finally sank out of sight.

❀

"That was a fine contraption," said Acise. Oh'Dar sighed and turned to thank his helpers before walking back to the village with her and Noshoba.

When they reached home, he told Acise, "I have

to go to Kthama now. All those materials are no doubt piled up somewhere, most likely in the Great Entrance or the Great Chamber. Do you still want to come with me?"

"Of course!" she answered. "Let me get a few things, and I will be right along."

Oh'Dar and Acise arrived at Kthama after dark. The cold clear night had revealed all the twinkling stars overhead, and the full moon lit their path. They had walked hand in hand where they could and single file where they could not. Simply happy to be together, they spent most of the walk in companionable silence.

Once inside the Great Entrance, Oh'Dar went over to the pile of items. He was relieved to see that everything had been set down far away from the moisture-dripping stalactites overhead. *I should have known they would.* Briefly, he reflected that there would not be any simple way to get more supplies with the wagon gone. His grandmother would simply have told him to buy another one, and he would have to if he needed to bring anything else cumbersome from Wilde Edge. *Oh well. Nothing I can do about it now.*

He turned to Acise, "Come on, it is late. Now that I know everything is safe, I can deal with it in the morning."

After disturbing his parents briefly, Oh'Dar took Acise's hand and led her to their Kthama quarters. His gaze traveled over the familiar walls and his feet welcomed the feel of the rock floors.

Oh'Dar opened the wooden door of their quarters, and they stepped inside. Both sank into the puffy bed, and for a moment, he simply stretched out next to Acise. Then he turned, remembering her promise for their night together, only to find her sound asleep. He leaned across to pull the hide blanket over them, and his last thought before he drifted off to sleep was *home. Home again at last.*

News of the exciting pile of items in the Great Entrance had quickly traveled through Kthama. Many walked around the perimeter, not touching but trying their best to peer into the middle to see everything. Most of it was packed up, however, which thwarted their curiosity. They talked among themselves about several of the unwrapped items, trying to imagine their purpose.

After a night of much-needed rest, as Oh'Dar and Acise walked into the Great Entrance, several of the older offspring came running over. "What is this? And this? And what is in *this*?" they asked, pointing to various objects in the pile.

"You will all see soon enough," Oh'Dar chuckled. "But some of it is a surprise for my grandparents!"

Then he looked around. "Is Nasha here?" Nasha poked her head out and squeezed her way to the front.

"Here I am," she smiled.

"I need your help. You and Snaven. Where is Snaven?"

The offspring raised her hand.

"Great. I need you both to keep my grandparents busy for a while this morning. Do you think you could do that? Starting after first meal?"

"Oh, yes, Oh'Dar," they chimed together. "We can do that!"

"Thank you. Later on, I will tell you what this is about, but for now, I just need you to keep Miss Vivian and Ben busy."

Nasha, Snaven, and a few others all nodded and scampered off to the Great Chambers, hoping to find the grandparents and get on with helping Oh'Dar.

"I am also curious to see what this is about," said Acise.

"You will. I just pray it does what I think it should."

A flurry of activity took place while Nasha and Snaven had Oh'Dar's grandparents distracted.

It was not a difficult task to keep them busy, as Miss Vivian and Ben had promised to spend time teaching the class the Waschini names for more of

Etera's creatures. It had turned into a type of game, with each offspring coming to the front, and with the chalk, drawing an animal for which he or she gave the People's name, after which Ben or Miss Vivian spoke the Waschini name and wrote it out. Then the young ones took turns mimicking the Waschini pronunciation, and in turn, Ben and Miss Vivian tried the People's word for the animal. It was great fun as sometimes the offspring argued over what animal had just been drawn. Ben and Miss Vivian smiled at the commotion as one or another tweaked the drawing until it better resembled what it was supposed to be, and consensus was reached.

Under Oh'Dar's direction, a group of females, including Adia and Acise, helped to finish up the finer touches after the males had done their part. Finally, Oh'Dar stepped back and surveyed the scene.

He put an arm around Acise and kissed the top of her head. He put his other arm around his mother's waist.

"They are going to love it. I see now," Acise said. "It reminds me of how my mother described her childhood in the Waschini house, though I imagined it a bit differently."

"One last thing," Oh'Dar said. And he walked across the room and fiddled with a wooden contraption sitting on top of one of the new items he had brought in.

The females exchanged questioning glances and then looked at what Oh'Dar had done.

Tick, tick, tick. The sound of the mantle clock that had sat on the top of the sideboard in the dining room at Shadow Ridge was the perfect finishing touch.

"What is that?" Adia asked.

"It is what they call a clock. See these little metal sticks. They move around this flat round thing with the symbols on it, and they mark time. From them, the Waschini can tell what time it is," he tried to explain.

"Time? How can you mark time? It is always moving," said Adia. "And where would you start? Time has always been, has it not?"

"It is a strange concept," he agreed. "Someday, I will try to find a better way to explain it."

One of the females who had moved outside to stand watch poked her head back in. "They are coming!"

She stepped in, and all the females moved into the food preparation area, which had not been part of the transformation. They were just in time for Oh'Dar's grandparents to enter.

Miss Vivian's hands flew to her mouth. "Oh my," she exclaimed. "Oh my," she said again as she looked around the room.

The first, most obvious thing was the fine

wooden bedstead and soft covered mattress that had replaced their sleeping mat. Then she turned to the wooden dresser, upon which was perched her favorite teacup. Next to the bed was a nightstand, on top of which Ben's reading glasses lay beside an oil lamp. On the other side of the bed, a set of lace curtains was attached to the rock wall. Though there was no window behind them, it gave the appearance that there was. It was oddly comforting.

Miss Vivian turned to Oh'Dar with tears in her eyes. "You did this? You brought all of this back from Wilde Edge?" she stammered.

Oh'Dar wrapped his arms around his grandmother. "I know it's not as fine as Shadow Ridge, but I'm hoping it will help some," he said into her ear.

She pulled away and looked over at her husband.

"Oh, Ben. Look what Oh'Dar did." Then she turned to the others in the room. "What you all did. Oh, thank you so much!"

Some in the room understood her Waschini words. Those who did not, needed no translation. They could see how happy she was, and they were glad to have been a part of bringing Oh'Dar's grandparents such joy.

Ben put an arm around Oh'Dar's shoulder. "Thank you for doing this for us."

"Wait," Miss Vivian said. She held a finger up as if signaling for silence. Then she spotted the clock on the low dresser at the other side of the room.

"It's running!" she exclaimed. Some of the females looked at each other in confusion.

"Of course, we have no idea what time it really is," she said as she walked over to the mantle clock. "Perhaps that's just as well. I see now how structured our lives were. Out of rhythm with the natural order of life, now that I know better. But I do cherish the familiar sound. Thank you again, everyone," she said.

Mapiya rounded up the females except for Adia and Acise and shooed them out, wanting to give the grandparents a chance to enjoy their surprise without a crowd watching them.

After everyone had taken another look at the new things, Miss Vivian reached across and touched her daughter-in-law's hand. "How are you feeling? Is everything alright?"

"Yes, I feel fine. I have no problems at all," Acise answered.

Once they were finally alone, Ben and Miss Vivian went over and sat on their new bed.

"So this is why he had to take the wagon," said Ben.

"I hate to admit it, but I'm so happy to have a real bed again," Miss Vivian smiled. "And a mattress!"

"Of all the things he could have brought us, I think it was the most helpful. Oh, and the oil lamp,"

Ben added. "What a comfort it will be in the dark of night."

"I'll be anxious to get back here tonight now." She ran her hands over the smooth linens and soft blankets.

"How much we took for granted," said Ben. "And despite this, how much we didn't really need at all to be happy."

Miss Vivian got up from the bed and went over to her beloved clock. She fingered the fine dresser scarf on which it was resting. Curious, she slid open one of the drawers to find an assortment of yarns and some knitting needles. "Oh," she exclaimed. "Mrs. Thomas must have told Grayson that I used to knit. What a nice surprise. And look, writing paper, a little ink well, and some quills!"

Holding up one of the quills, she turned back to Ben, who was still sitting on the bed. "Perhaps I should start a journal," she mused.

"That's a good idea. It would be interesting someday in the future to go back and remember how it was when we first came here."

Miss Vivian replaced the quill and picked up a little paper bag. She peeked inside, "Oh Ben, it's your favorite hard licorice candy!" She replaced the little bag and slid the drawer closed.

"Now we can stop living out of those trunks," she exclaimed. "Tomorrow, we can take out what we brought, go through it, and organize it properly. That in itself will be a great relief."

Miss Vivian returned to the bed and sat down beside her husband. "Are you still happy we came?" she asked.

Ben reached up and smoothed from her forehead a stray strand of beautiful auburn hair. "Yes, I am. Here, I have a chance at doing something no one else has ever done. Even though no one will ever know, and even if we had anyone to tell, they'd never believe us. I don't yet understand all that's truly going on here; it will take time. But that does not take away from its importance. Oh, my dear, what an adventure, yes?"

Miss Vivian leaned over and sweetly kissed him. "Yes. And Grayson's wife is with child! Soon there will be another little Morgan running about. Oh, I can't wait to hold him—or her!"

Their conversation was interrupted by the clack of the announcement stone.

"Come in!" Miss Vivian called out, knowing that the People now recognized that phrase as permission to enter.

Pakuna stuck her head in and made the sign for eating. Miss Vivian nodded and smiled, and Pakuna retreated. It was time to join the others at evening meal.

The People were adjusting to the grandparents' presence. Mothers and fathers had quickly corrected their offspring, who had now stopped continually visiting their table and interrupting their meal. Ben and Miss Vivian welcomed the visits, but the parents were concerned it would become annoying over time.

That evening, however, the Waschini grandparents were not the center of attention. Instead, everyone was focused on the presence of a tall, muscular, and remarkably handsome male who wore a stylized hide cape of some type and had joined Acaraho and Adia at their table.

"Who's that?" Miss Vivian whispered to Oh'Dar.

"That's Khon'Tor. He was the Leader here and is visiting for a while."

"He and your father look similar," said Ben. "Except this one has that striking white streak running from his crown toward the back of his head."

"They're related. Both are of the House of 'Tor," Oh'Dar explained.

The rest of the evening was spent in pleasant conversation, during which Oh'Dar explained that before too long, a High Council meeting would be held at Kthama. Ben and Miss Vivian understood the concept and seemed excited at the thought of seeing such a gathering of the People's Leaders. When he explained that it would include the Brothers' Leaders, their excitement doubled.

"I found the knitting and writing materials; thank you," Miss Vivian added.

"That's not all I brought back. Tomorrow I'll show you where the rest is stored, along with oil for your lamp. There's more than enough to last for years. If you remember, I said I was asked to write down the People's history, so it's no longer only passed along by word of mouth. The one you noticed, Khon'Tor, he's the one who asked for this. He stressed that it needed to be accurate and not censored or edited in any way."

"So there are some aspects which are perhaps not flattering to particular people?" she asked.

"Yes. And I was thinking, Grandmother, that perhaps the best person to do this would be you. These writings are meant for the future, that the coming generations will know the truth of what happened. That's why my people have to learn what we call Whitespeak. They have to learn to speak and write as we do, then they won't be held hostage to stories that have been twisted or partially forgotten over time. The white language is complex, able to express in great detail. The People's written markings are general and carry only a rough outline of concepts."

"We understand, son," Ben said. "From what you told us on the trip here, there was tremendous misunderstanding about the past."

"Yes. But the truth can be unflattering—painful even. Grandmother, you'd be neutral. You wouldn't even know most of the individuals, so those telling their story would be far less guarded."

Miss Vivian reached across the table and laid her hand on her grandson's arm. "Whatever I can do to help you, I will."

That settled, Oh'Dar explained that he and Acise would be returning to the village for a while but that he would be back for the High Council meeting.

At the close of the meal, Ben and Miss Vivian were happy to return to their quarters for their first night's sleep in their new bed.

⟨🐾⟩

The next morning, Oh'Dar spoke to Acaraho. "I have been thinking. My grandmother will start writing down our history; I brought more than enough materials to keep her busy for some time. However, part of that history is written on The Wall of Records."

"You are suggesting it is time they visit the Wall of Records? That means we must introduce him to Bidzel and Yuma'qia. I will make arrangements. We can go anytime you think they are ready."

⟨🐾⟩

Acaraho led the way, and Miss Vivian, Ben, Oh'Dar, and Khon'Tor followed. Ben held Miss Vivian's arm to steady her along the snow-covered path. Finally, they stood at Kht'shWea's entrance.

Haan and First Rank, Haaka, waited inside to greet them. Out of courtesy, Haan had ordered the entrance and corridors cleared except for essential workers.

Ben and Miss Vivian tried to contain their shock

when they saw Haan and Haaka standing side by side. They had seen Notar only at night and then at a distance. All the detail hidden in the dark was now evident even in the dimmer cave light. The hulking shoulders, the thick, full-bodied coat that gave an illusion of green undertones, the large head, and the dark, deep-set eyes, the long muscular arms that ended in huge hands. There seemed little noticeable difference between the two, except that one was smaller, and there was some hint of breasts under her heavy covering.

Oh'Dar translated as Haan issued a greeting before motioning toward the hallway, and they all followed. The soft sand accumulated through the ages was still underfoot, left there by the Sarnonn out of respect for the Ancients.

Before long, they could see an overhead shaft of light that revealed a large entrance. Bidzel and Yuma'qia were waiting outside it, and Oh'Dar introduced them to his grandparents. Then the two researchers stood back, and Ben and Miss Vivian stepped past them and stopped.

Ben squeezed his eyes shut and opened them, checking that he had indeed seen what he thought he had. Floor to ceiling, left to right, pictographs and symbols covered walls of spell-binding height. A considerable scaffolding of whole tree trunks, saplings, and branches was spread across part of the expanse. Steps reached up multiple levels, Ben realized, to give the researchers access.

"This is the Wall of Records," explained Haan. "The complete recording of the Age of Wrak-Wavara, The Age of Darkness. It was during this period the Fathers-Of-Us-All betrayed the trust of the Others—those you know as the Brothers. Through this betrayal were born the Akassa and the Sassen. For our own good, we were kept apart through the ages, but now we are reunited as one people and work together to create a future of our own making."

Oh'Dar continued to translate as Haan turned to address Ben directly. "Adik'Tar Acaraho tells us you are a great researcher in your own right. It is our fervent prayer that the Great Spirit has brought you here to help us solve the problem facing us. For if we do not, then both the Sassen and the Akassa will vanish from Etera."

"I'll do my best to help you," promised Ben.

"That is all that can be asked of anyone," Haan replied.

Ben turned to Miss Vivian, "I'd like to stay awhile and study the markings."

She nodded and patted her husband's arm.

Oh'Dar offered to stay and continue translating.

Haan then turned to Khon'Tor, "It is good to see you, Adik'Tar. You are welcome to stay with us as long as you wish."

"Thank you, Adik'Tar," Khon'Tor replied.

Haaka offered to show him to his living space, explaining that Sastak would tend to his needs while he was there.

Adia and Acaraho returned to Kthama as much planning was underway for the arrival of the High Council members. Miss Vivian happily accompanied them.

A guard approached Acaraho, "I have a message for you from Larara, mate of the previous Overseer."

Acaraho gave a nod and waited.

"She has asked to come to the High Council meeting. She is petitioning for Bak'tah-Awhidi."

Acaraho glanced at Adia and was silent for a moment. "She is welcome to come. We will address her request privately."

When the guard had left, Adia spoke. "Not unexpected."

"No doubt. But this seems to suggest that Kurak'Kahn is not accepting Khon'Tor's punishment. I doubt he ever will, really."

"Even with Berak's body being found, Larara and Linoi's parents must still be suffering greatly," she said. "The offspring is out there somewhere. I believe this. No—I know it."

"I trust you. But that means someone is caring for U'Kail. It would have to be one of the Brothers' tribes with which none of our communities is associated. Otherwise, I am certain that someone would have approached us by now," Acaraho said.

"Perhaps it would be appropriate to bring this

before the High Council? They may know of other villages or camps where he might be," she suggested. "I will speak with Larara when she arrives and get her blessing."

Acaraho nodded. He had drawn a representation of Kthama on a piece of birch bark and now returned to it. He was moving the stones around his depiction of the levels, living quarters, and other rooms in an attempt to figure out temporary living arrangements for their guests. Inviting the Healers and Helpers and the Brothers' Chiefs brought the attendance almost to Ashwea Awhidi proportions.

Adia let out a long sigh. "I miss Urilla Wuti. I am so looking forward to seeing her." *Has she had any visits with E'ranale? What has she learned about Nootau's abilities? Will there always be more questions than answers?* she wondered.

The next morning, Khon'Tor left Kht'shWea for Kthama. On the way, he pondered his situation. *Why am I being sent here? Because Urilla Wuti and Harak'Sar got some notion that something is afoot of which I need to be aware. Their continued trust surprises me.*

The cold snow crunched under his feet as he walked. Fresh snow was starting to fall and dusted his shoulders. *Soon the entire High Council will arrive. Faces, other Leaders whom I have not seen in decades. We should not have let it go this long.*

As he walked into the Great Entrance, Khon'Tor stomped his feet and brushed the snow from his hide cloak. The guards along the perimeter turned to look and stopped talking. They started to approach him but then hesitated, not sure what was now proper.

He waved them off and continued through to the Great Chamber where most would be at the morning meal. As he walked, several young males came up and excitedly chattered to him. He saw the admiration in their eyes and let himself take solace in it. Several of them even walked backward so they could continue to look at him as they talked. Finally, he stopped to answer their questions, which were mostly about whether he had returned to Kthama for good. He gently explained that he was only visiting and reminded them that their Leader was now Acaraho'Tor.

"We meant no disrespect to Adik'Tar Acaraho," said one.

Khon'Tor nodded and continued over to the table occupied by Nootau, Acaraho, and Adia. Acaraho motioned for him to sit, and Mapiya soon brought him a selection of the morning's offerings.

"The first visitors will arrive this afternoon," said Acaraho. "The morning after next, we should be ready to start."

"It has been a long time since the whole High Council has met together," observed Khon'Tor. "The last one I attended was with Chief Ogima when we first discussed the Waschini threat. Many extraordinary events have taken place since then."

"There is much information to share, but we also need to listen," replied Acaraho. "We know nothing of what is going on with the Brothers' communities, other than Chief Is'Taqa's. I am allowing quite a bit of time for that. No doubt, the news of the Sarnonn will come as a surprise to many of them. There have been rumors of their existence, but as far as we know, we are the only ones who have had immediate contact with them."

"You are asking Haan to speak?" asked Khon'Tor.

"Yes. The Brothers need to know we have forged a bond of friendship and that it is also extended to them," Acaraho answered.

"And what of Oh'Dar's grandparents?" Khon'Tor asked.

"They will also be there. And the Sarnonn Guardians, and—" Acaraho looked at his mate. "And An'Kru."

He then turned to Khon'Tor, "As you have said, the time for secrets must end. If we cannot trust them with the truth, then our alliance is an illusion. A storm is coming. Something more important than anything we have been through yet. I know that sounds dramatic as we have been through so much already. But I think we all feel it—in our bones, in our souls. We all know, through our connection with the Great Spirit. Something is coming, something for which we cannot prepare, and yet, somehow, we must. It will take all of us working together to prepare for what yet lies ahead."

As Adia turned An'Kru around and tucked him inside her wrap to nurse, Khon'Tor glanced at the tiny offspring, then back at Acaraho. "He is the key."

"Yes. Somehow, An'Kru is the key. But he is not all of it. There are other pivotal figures. I now believe you are one of them," Acaraho said, staring at Khon'Tor.

Khon'Tor looked away and almost said something cynical about himself before realizing the others were probably becoming as tired of his self-disparagement as he was. He ran his hand through his hair. *Find your way. Move on. What is done is done. Tehya deserves more. She deserves someone present and engaged in this life, not constantly bemoaning mistakes of the past. You are of no use to anyone like this.*

He looked back to see Acaraho studying him.

"You are, and always have been, a wise and powerful speaker," said the new Leader. "I trust your judgment. If you feel called to address the High Council, do not hold back. I am asking you." His eyes never wavered from Khon'Tor's.

"How have you laid everything out?" Khon'Tor finally asked, and Acaraho went through the planned order of events with the former Leader of the High Rocks.

CHAPTER 10

Newall Storis ripped open the envelope, hoping it was the news he was waiting for. Inside, scrawled clumsily across a previously used scrap of paper, were the words *I have information you want. Bring payment.*

Storis crumpled it up and tossed it into the trash can before packing the papers on his desk and closing his shop. He was on his way back to Wilde Edge.

Tucker was waiting for him in the usual spot, the seedy drinking establishment on the far edge of town. Storis walked directly over to him.

"I'm here. So tell me what I want to know."

"Is that how you treat your employee?" snarled Tucker. "Not even offering to buy me a drink?"

Storis frowned and walked over to the bar, where he handed the barkeeper a coin and tilted his head in Tucker's direction.

The barkeeper slammed a glass on the bar and filled it with whiskey. Tucker wandered over, picked up the shot, and downed it.

"Another," he said, sneering at the lawyer.

Storis nodded to the barkeeper, who poured a second one.

"Ahhhhh," Tucker sighed as he threw back the second shot.

"Alright, get on with it. You must have found him and followed him, correct?"

"I did. Tall, straight black hair, came in on a wagon with a fine team of bays, just like you said. And I can take you right to him."

"How far?"

"About a five-day ride."

"Tell me where he went," said Storis.

"Pay me what you told me you would, and I'll take you there myself," was the answer.

Storis thought a moment, realizing that traveling cross-country with no idea where he was going was a ridiculous thought. "I'll pay you half of what I promised you and the rest when we get there. That's the best I'll offer you," he said.

"Alright then. Meet me here in the morning. Rest tonight because it's going to be a tough journey. Can you hunt?"

"Well enough," Storis said.

"If your well enough isn't good enough, you're going to starve, so if you aren't sure about it, better stock up on some supplies for the road. You can rent a horse over at the livery. And don't forget to buy a feedbag and some grain as the grazing this time of year will be sparse. It isn't a properly marked route like that from Shadow Ridge, and there aren't any settlements along the way. I highly doubt you've any experience with a trip like this." And Tucker looked him up and down with another sneer.

"I'll settle with you in the morning," said Storis. "Before then, I have some friends I want to check up on." He laid another coin on the bar and walked out.

Storis set off to the Webb place. The cold air cleared his mind, and he went over the plan of what he was to do next.

He walked up the steps in front of the Webbs' house and knocked on the door. Within a moment, Mrs. Webb had opened it. "Well, Mr. Storis, how nice. Please come in." She stepped out of the way.

He removed his hat, stomped the snow from his boots, and walked in. The warm air was comforting and the smell from the kitchen delightful. A moment later, Grace popped around the corner.

"What are you doing here?" she asked.

"Grace!" Mrs. Webb exclaimed. "Really, is that how a young lady speaks?"

"It's alright." Storis couldn't stop himself from glancing at Grace as he spoke. "I'm passing through, and I wanted to make sure that everything was fine with the bank and the other arrangements Mr. Morgan had me make. Are you having any trouble with any of it?"

"No, no, thank you, none at all," replied Mrs. Webb. "Will you join us in the kitchen? We have just finished making dinner. You will stay, of course?"

"Oh, no, I should get back to town and get a room." He was embarrassed to say this as it sounded exactly like the last time he was there.

"Fiddlesticks, you'll stay with us as you did before. Grace, please call your father and brother to wash up for dinner."

Just as they were sitting down, there was a knock at the door. "Gracious, we never have visitors, and today we get two?" Mrs. Webb laid her napkin on the table, got up, and went to the door.

She opened it to a tall stranger who loomed above her. "I'm looking for a friend of mine, Storis. Is he here?"

"Why, yes, he is. Please come on in."

The stranger stepped inside, and Mrs. Webb showed him into the kitchen. In the corner, Buster growled.

"Mr. Storis, a friend of yours is here," she said as they entered the room. "A Mr.—"

"Tucker, Snide Tucker, ma'am," he said, belatedly removing his hat. "Snide's not my given name," he added.

Mrs. Webb now recognized him as being around town occasionally, usually hanging out near the bar.

He always looked unkempt, and she'd felt he had a mean edge to him. He was old man Rusty Tucker's boy and had either inherited or taken up his father's bad temperament.

Storis stared at the tracker, and for a moment, couldn't figure out what to say that wouldn't alarm the Webbs. Tucker was certainly no friend of his, and he could think of no valid reason for the man's arrival.

"Well, sit down and eat with us then, since you're here," said Mr. Webb. Ned jumped up to get a plate for the stranger and moved his chair over to make room. Tucker flopped his hat down on the sideboard.

"Sorry for the intrusion, Ma'am," he said. "Mr. Storis, we neglected to say what time we were meeting in the morning. I do recommend we get an early start."

"What time do you suggest?" Storis queried, a little too curtly.

"Daybreak is fine with me." Then Tucker started to help himself to the food on the table. Over the next hour, he pried out of the Webbs every bit of information he could. While they were talking, he kept eyeing Grace, a fact not lost on Storis.

"So, how do you know each other?" asked Mr. Webb.

"Oh, we're business partners," Tucker quickly replied. "We're about to go out of town on a business trip. Should be gone a couple of weeks. I'd be glad to stop by on the way back through," he added.

Storis saw Mrs. Webb glance at her husband and realized that this line of conversation and questioning was starting to worry them.

Though he was not finished, Storis pushed his chair back and laid his napkin on the table.

"Excuse me, Ma'am. Tucker, you'd best get going if we're each to have that good night's sleep you mentioned. Let me show you to the door." Storis picked up Tucker's hat from the sideboard and practically strong-armed him out.

Once outside, Tucker shrugged off Storis' grasp.

The lawyer closed the door behind them, "What are you doing? Why did you follow me here? And what was all that about in there? I've half a mind to pay you right now and be done with the whole thing," he hissed.

"Calm down; I'm just being friendly. Nothing wrong with that," Tucker snarled back. "You can be done with it, but you'll have wasted your trip here. I wasn't lying; I saw the man, and I know just where he is. So, are you sure you want to leave it?"

Storis huffed. "I'll meet you at daybreak. But you're never to come back to this house again. You understand?"

"Or what? You'll pull some lawyer move on me? The hell you will. But alright then, I'll see you in the morning."

Storis stood on the porch and waited a long time, watching Tucker until he was totally out of sight.

The lawyer let himself back into the house and

went into the kitchen, "I apologize about that, folks. Mr. Tucker is a business associate, but after this deal, we're done. I have no need to bother with him again. Now, with your permission, I'll retire. I have a long trip ahead of me and a lot on my mind."

Needless to say, he didn't sleep well.

⚜

Having had lots of time to think about it overnight, Storis was prepared. He met Tucker in town in front of the bar as agreed. "Here," he said, holding out a bag of coins. "Here's your payment. All of it."

Tucker snatched the bag from Storis' hand. "What does this mean?"

"Tell me where he went. I'll find it myself."

"There's no way you will," Tucker scoffed. "But have it your way. Head east for about three days and cross two streams; they're small, and with most everything freezing up by now, they shouldn't give you much trouble. After you pass the second stream, head North East for about a day. There's a local village there. That's where he went."

What I suspected, thought Storis. *It has to be the same village that was searched after Grayson and Rachel Morgan were murdered. I'm sure I can find someone else to help me find it. Someone more trustworthy than this fellow.*

Tucker studied Storis' face before saying, "Look. You'll never find it. You've no idea how to survive out there. You'll need supplies for yourself and the horse. Even though we haven't had a hard frost and the snow still comes and goes, it's a rough journey for a horse this time of year. I know I come off wrong, but a deal is a deal. I'll take you. At least get you far enough that you can't miss it."

Storis looked Tucker in the eye. *I don't like it. Somehow there's a double-cross, but he's right. I don't know anything about horses. Nor about surviving in the wild. Besides, if I leave him here, he may continue to hang around the Webbs. And I didn't like the way he looked at Grace.* "Alright. But only until there's no doubt I can find the rest of the way myself. Then you must wait until I return, and we'll head back. I don't want you anywhere near the village. Understood?"

Tucker chuckled.

"Agree to it, do as I say, and I'll pay you extra when we return."

Tucker spat off to the side before nodding his agreement. "Yes, alright."

Notar had been drinking from the nearby stream, and he stood up to an unusual amount of commotion. He turned to see his Healer and several other males carrying a limp body. He quickly flicked the water off his hand and stormed over to them.

"What has happened? Is that Nit? Is he dead?"

"Yes," replied the Healer.

"Put him down," ordered Notar.

The males gently laid Nit on the ground.

Notar stooped down to examine him, first turning Nit's limp head side to side and then searching the bloodied fur for an injury site. "What is this? Where is the blood coming from? This hole? What caused this?"

One of the males spoke up. "I was with him. We were foraging, and Nit stepped out of the brush. There was a Waschini, and I think Nit's sudden appearance startled him. He had a long stick. He held it up to his face—like this. Then there was a loud sound, almost like a tree makes when it cracks at the base, and Nit grabbed his chest and fell down. The Waschini came over to look at him, but I came out of the brush and scared him off. I do not know why he did not use the stick on me. But it was too late for Nit."

"We hardly ever see them. What would one be doing here?"

"He was covered in hides, and he looked as if he was used to being out here. He was upwind, or we would have noticed him. Is it no longer safe here for us?" asked the male who had been with Nit.

Notar rubbed his face with both hands, thinking. "You were careless. Now Nit is gone, and you have been seen by a Waschini. The Waschini must not know of our existence. If they do, no doubt they will hunt us to extinction as they do all other creatures. And how am I to tell Lezuan that her offling has returned to the Great Spirit?" He scanned the far horizon as if looking for wisdom. "We must all pray to the Great Spirit for guidance, but for now, let us take him home and prepare his Good Journey."

They gently lifted the giant shaggy body off the ground and headed back home.

As they stooped down to pass through the low entrance and entered their cave system, those there gathered around and stood staring at the limp body of Nit. One of the females ran to get Lezuan and led her in by the hand, then stood with her arms around Nit's mother as she took in what had happened. Once Lezuan realized who it was dangling in Notar's arms, she ran forward and hugged the body of her dead son, wailing as the others present shook their heads. When Lezuan's mate entered, he beat his chest in anguish and also wailed loudly at the loss of their only offling.

Notar's community grieved with Nit's parents over their personal loss, but to lose an unpaired adult who had not yet reproduced was also a blow to their population. As they conducted the Good Journey ritual, Notar could not help but worry again about the future of their bloodlines. Despite Pan's very recent appearance to him, he was struggling to maintain his faith in The Order of Functions.

CHAPTER 11

Acise had gone back home a few days earlier, and Oh'Dar was anxious. He wanted to return to the village to check on her. However, nearly everyone was busily occupied with the upcoming High Council visit, and he knew he had to prepare his grandparents beforehand.

He first had to consult his parents, and eventually, he found them together in the Leader's Quarters.

Adia gave him a hug. "Here, could you hold An'Kru for a moment while I finish this last knot?" She was taking a quick break to work on a new sling for him, simply because it pleased her to do so.

Oh'Dar took An'Kru and held him for a moment. The offspring's little feet dangled free, and he smiled up at Oh'Dar.

"He is such a happy soul!" Oh'Dar exclaimed. "And look at his eyes!"

Adia chuckled, "That is exactly what everyone said about you."

"Well, I think he is fascinating. And he is part of what I wanted to speak to you both about," he said as he cradled An'Kru in his arms.

"My grandparents are going to be at some of the High Council assemblies, right? They have met the Sarnonn and the Brothers, but there are still those who are—different? I do not mean to sound rude—"

Acaraho rescued him. "You are talking about An'Kru and the Guardians."

"Yes, Father, I am."

"I agree," nodded Acaraho. "Ben and Miss Vivian need to meet them ahead of time, and so far, your grandparents have only met Haan and Haaka. Their first experience of being among a group of Sarnonn should not take place in a crowded room."

"What are they occupied with today?" Adia asked, pulling the knot as tight as she could. She then looped it over her shoulder and let it rest on the front of her hip. "There. Hand him back to me, please," she said as she reached for An'Kru. Oh'Dar gave him back, and Adia placed him in the sling. He looked up and smiled again.

"I think Grandmother is finally taking a break," Oh'Dar answered, peering down at An'Kru snug in his little holder. "Ben is probably back at the Wall of Records. Even though he and Bidzel and Yuma'qia cannot communicate, he seems to be able to understand the patterns of the markings to quite an extent.

"Did I like being in a sling when I was little?" he asked.

"You and Nootau both," smiled his mother. "You both loved it. You, in particular, seemed to enjoy looking around to see what else you could take apart and put back together again." She chuckled. "Whenever you were able to, you were always reaching for something you should not have! Now, I am ready if you are. If you want to go and find your grandmother, we can meet you at the Wall of Records in a little bit."

Oh'Dar looked at his father, who nodded.

Before long, Adia and Acaraho were making their way to Kht'shWea with little An'Kru bundled up in a tiny wolf pelt in Adia's arms. The foot coverings felt good as she padded along the path. As always, a sense of reverence fell over her as she approached what used to be the Healer's Cove, now the opening to Kthama Minor.

Haan had told Acaraho and Adia they were always welcome at Kht'shWea and did not need to send a message ahead. The moment they walked in, High Protector Qirrik turned and signaled for one of the others to fetch Haan.

Accompanied by several males, the Sarnonn Leader appeared almost as if out of nowhere. "Welcome," he said as he walked over to them. Suddenly, he noticed that Adia held the offspring in her arms.

His gaze froze, and Adia gently uncovered the little face, at which Haan and the others each dropped to one knee and bowed their heads. As he had done when An'Kru was first introduced at Kthama, Haan slowly returned to his feet, raised one hand over his head, and announced, "An'Kru! The Promised One has come!" Then he bumped his fist over his heart.

The others also rose, although they simply stepped back.

"You honor us with your visit. What can we do for you?" Haan was still staring at the tiny offspring.

"We have a favor to ask," said Acaraho. "We would like Oh'Dar's grandparents to meet at least one of the Sarnonn Guardians. As you can imagine, they are going through a major transition, and with the High Council meeting coming up, we thought it would be better for them to know of the Guardians existence ahead of time. Oh'Dar is bringing his grandmother here now."

Haan nodded and turned to those behind him. He shouted out some orders, and two of them split off from the group.

"The grandfather is at the Wall of Records. He will be here soon, as will Thord or Lellaach."

"Thank you, Haan," said Acaraho.

"They have been anxious to see An'Kru, the Promised One. They will be overjoyed at this," Haan added.

A few moments later, Oh'Dar arrived with Miss Vivian. She was heavily bundled up in her Waschini overcoat, hat, and scarf. When she arrived, they all went together to one of the rooms not far from the entrance.

Once they were comfortable, Oh'Dar addressed his grandparents. "You know there will be many different people coming for the High Council meeting. Many will be our people who live here, and there will also be many of those who live in the communities farther away. Some will be Chiefs of the Brothers, and Haan and his people will also be there. There will be lots of announcements and much sharing of news. And there will be introductions to people whom many of the community don't yet know exist."

"Since we know you are already dealing with a lot, we wanted to soften what could be another difficult moment by preparing you ahead of time," Adia added softly.

Miss Vivian looked at Oh'Dar and raised her eyebrows.

"This is my offspring, An'Kru," Adia said. "He is revered by the Sarnonn because their prophecy foretold his coming. You will see his coloring is unlike any of ours." Adia gently pulled back the covering from An'Kru's face.

Miss Vivian let out a gasp, and Ben frowned and leaned forward. "What the—" He caught himself.

"Oh, my heavens," Miss Vivian exclaimed. "His beautiful eyes. And his hair." She looked up at Adia, "He's remarkable!"

Ben moved closer to Adia, "May I?" he asked

breathlessly, taking out his reading glasses and putting them on.

Adia carefully handed An'Kru to Ben, and the offspring immediately reached up toward Ben's glasses.

"This is your child? Yours and Acaraho's?" Ben asked.

Adia nodded.

"Does either of you have this coloring in your background?" he asked, looking first at Acaraho, then Adia.

"From what the researchers tell us, no," said Adia, answering for them both.

Ben looked at his wife and shook his head. "From everything I understand after years of working with breeding combinations, this shouldn't be possible. I'm sorry, but it just shouldn't," he stammered.

Haan came through the doorway with Thord and Lellaach behind him. Seeing the giant silver-white forms behind Haan, Ben handed An'Kru back to Adia and stumbled back to Miss Vivian.

"I have brought Thord and Lellaach, Leaders of the Sarnonn Guardians," Haan announced.

Oh'Dar said to his grandparents, "I'll explain about the Guardians later," to which Ben quickly nodded.

Haan stepped into the room to allow Thord and Lellaach to enter. As Haan had done, the moment they spotted An'Kru in Adia's arms, both dropped to one knee. They then rose and pounded their fists over their hearts in what Adia and the others now recognized as a gesture meant for the offspring.

"Are the others coming?" asked Oh'Dar.

"There are more like them?" asked his grandmother, staring at the silver-coated behemoths standing in front of them.

"There are twelve in total," explained Adia.

Haan said, "The twelve cannot be in the presence of the An'Kru, The Promised One, until the appointed time. The prophecy strongly prohibits this until they have been prepared to engage in the Ror'Eckrah. We must work together to make sure they are never all in the same room at one time."

"The One Mind," Oh'Dar translated. "My mother explained that it is a type of trance that they go into from which they can summon tremendous power."

Adia's frustration rose. "Pieces of the mystery but never the whole story," she whispered under her breath to her mate.

"So much to learn," said Ben, who was trying not to stare at Thord and Lellaach.

Finally, Acaraho thanked everyone. "I believe we can all get back to what we were doing." He turned to Oh'Dar, who was helping Miss Vivian to her feet.

"May I hold him sometime?" Miss Vivian asked Adia, who was still sitting.

"Of course. Here," Adia answered and handed over An'Kru.

Miss Vivian looked down at the little offling and

rearranged his bundling so she could see his face better. "Oh. He's so sweet!" she exclaimed.

"Before you leave," said Haan. "The six Guardian females are all with offling. I thought you might want to know."

Adia stared at him. "All six? All at the same time?"

Haan nodded.

Adia looked up at her mate, "I need to speak with Urilla Wuti the moment she arrives, please."

"Of course, Saraste.'"

Ben decided to return to his work with Bidzel and Yuma'qia at the Wall of Records and asked if Oh'Dar could stay awhile and translate as his questions were piling up. Oh'Dar agreed, and Acaraho said they would again escort Miss Vivian, who wanted to rest in the quarters at Kthama.

As they left through Kht'shWea's entrance, Adia looked back to see a semi-circle of Sarnonn lined up and watching them leave.

Safely back in her room, Miss Vivian took out another piece of paper and wrote about the day's events. She knew that no one would ever read the entries and that, even if they did, they would not believe such a fantastical story. *But it helps me to write it down, anyway.*

CHAPTER 12

As well as he could, Storis dressed according to Tucker's instructions. He rented a horse from the local livery but had to pay a premium due to the keeper's concern about the horse's welfare. That and the money Tucker said he needed to pay for supplies had drained his pockets.

Tucker pulled up at the appointed time, and Storis looked at the small wagon hitched up behind the horse. "What's that for?"

"Food for the horses. They can graze a bit if we don't get any deep snow, but they'll need more than that. Since there aren't any towns between here and where we're going, I had to bring enough for the whole trip. Also, they need about ten gallons of water a day, hence the barrels. There won't always be a river or stream handy."

"Isn't that going to slow us down?" Storis asked.

"Not as much as a dead horse would. Come on, let's get going."

Despite fair weather, the trip was still grueling. The men had to make many stops to care for the horses. The nights were bitterly cold, and only the thought of one of the animals dying kept Storis from stealing their blankets to add to his.

While Tucker was caring for the horses, Storis would pull out a small writing pad and make notes along the way. He made sure to tuck it back into his jacket pocket before Tucker caught him at it.

The days and nights passed. Storis was in a perpetual state of hunger and cold. He suspected Tucker was sneaking food and eating more than his share as the man never seemed to complain about not having enough to eat.

He won't get paid anything more if I don't survive, and he knows this. I guess he's just a mean, spiteful individual. For some reason, he resents me and wants me to suffer.

A winter hunting party returned to the village, and after Isskel had dismounted, he immediately went to Chief Is'Taqa.

"Two Waschini riders are approaching the far ridge. They appear to be setting up for the night," Isskel told him.

Pajackok had been talking to the Chief, and after some discussion, sprang to his feet.

With Pajackok leading them, Isskel and two other braves approached the Waschini men. A pair of horses and a small Waschini wagon were tethered to the trees some distance away.

The man who first saw them called out to the other, who walked over to the Brothers.

He looked Pajackok squarely in the eye, raised his hand to show height, and pulled his fingers straight down both sides of his face to indicate long, straight hair. Then he pointed to his eyes, to the blue sky, and back again.

Pajackok glanced at the other riders. "He is looking for Oh'Dar."

"They look terrible," said one of the braves. "And I can smell them from here!"

Pajackok brought Atori up closer to the man. He made the same gestures back, then pointed in the direction of their village.

The man in the background nodded wildly and stepped forward, his hands outstretched. He pointed at himself and then in the direction Pajackok had indicated.

"He wants us to take him to Oh'Dar," Isskel said unnecessarily.

Pajackok circled Atori and motioned for the men to follow. They all waited while the two Waschini conversed.

"I'm going with them, and you can wait here. That was the deal," said Storis.

Tucker scowled at him, "Alright. But if you aren't back soon, I'm leaving without you. I don't have enough supplies for both of us if I must wait too long. Although, if something happens to you, I'll have more than enough."

"Yes, but no money, so don't get any ideas. And don't follow us; this is none of your business, and I'll make it as quick as I can."

And so Storis remounted his horse and followed the braves.

Tucker paced around a bit, collecting more firewood, then angrily kicked at those he'd stacked.

The village activity came to a standstill when Pajackok, Isskel, and the other braves rode into town with a Waschini among them.

Mothers gathered their children and hurried them into the shelters. Chief Is'Taqa told Honovi, Acise, and Snana to take Noshoba and do the same, but shortly after, Honovi returned to Is'Taqa's side.

He frowned at her, to which she responded, "And just who is going to translate?"

Pajackok and the others remained on their horses while Storis dismounted and slowly walked over to the Chief. Not knowing what was appropriate, he bowed and started speaking very slowly.

He used the same gestures to describe Oh'Dar, at which Chief Is'Taqa looked sideways at Honovi, who nodded.

"Do you understand me at all? I need to see him. I know you know who I mean. He is tall with straight black hair. Eyes the color of the sky. Please, it is important. Where is he?" and Storis looked around.

"He does not look well; I pray he is not ill," said Honovi.

Chief Is'Taqa looked Storis up and down and said, "Tell him he can stay here with us. We will bring the one he seeks to him. But he is not to leave the shelter. He must wait patiently, and we will take care of him and his horse while he does."

Honovi spoke to Storis, whose eyes widened at hearing one of the locals speak English.

"You can understand me!"

"Yes, I can. Did you understand me?" Honovi asked. "Did you hear what our Chief just said?"

"Yes, yes. Thank you," said Storis.

One of the braves dismounted and took Storis' horse away to be looked after. Chief Is'Taqa ordered one of the other braves to locate a place for the Waschini to stay. Before long, Storis was sitting in front of a blazing fire, a fresh blanket around his shoulders, clutching a gourd of some type of stew and feeling very grateful for the kindness he was being shown.

Honovi and Is'Taqa stood in the background watching.

"He does not seem to be a threat, but what do we know of them? Can it be possible that he is someone Oh'Dar knows?" Honovi pondered.

"We must let Oh'Dar know he is here," Is'Taqa said. "I will send a message with one of the People's watchers."

"There is no room for misunderstanding," Honovi pointed out. "I shall write a message for one of their watchers to deliver."

A while later, Honovi stepped into the woods and whistled as Adia had taught several of the Brothers to do if they needed help from one of the People. Within a few moments, a huge form stepped out from around a tree trunk. He stood blinking, and Honovi stepped forward with the piece of birch bark. After a short conversation, the watcher nodded, and within moments, he was on his way with the message.

Oh'Dar stood holding the strip of bark on which Honovi had scribbled, "Waschini man called Storis here waiting for you."

He turned to his father. "I have to leave for the village. Now. My grandparent's lawyer—helper—has shown up looking for me!"

By the time Oh'Dar made it to the village, Storis had been able to get some rest. He'd been so exhausted from the trip and concern about Tucker's real motives in bringing him there that he'd ceased worrying about the villagers. They'd been nothing but kind to him.

He started when he heard someone enter the tent and looked up to see young Mr. Morgan towering over him.

"What are you doing here, Mr. Storis?" Oh'Dar asked.

Storis looked him up and down, noting that the young man no longer wore regular clothing but seemed dressed more like the locals than anything.

"Where are Miss Vivian and Ben Jenkins?" he demanded, rising to his feet.

"Is that why you've come?" Oh'Dar asked.

"I know they aren't dead, so don't waste my time. I delivered the paperwork you asked me to draw up for the Webbs, and they mentioned you'd stopped there and weren't alone. Now, where are they, and why did you fabricate their deaths?"

Having heard the raised voices, Chief Is'Taqa and Honovi also entered the shelter.

Oh'Dar turned to them and said in their language, "This man worked for my grandparents. He has come looking for them. But I cannot tell him where they are as it would only lead to more questions."

"Stop that," Storis said. "What are you saying? I demand you bring them to me at once. They're not here, so they must be staying with you somewhere else, or it wouldn't have taken you so long to arrive. Take me to them or bring them to this village; either way, I'm not leaving until I see them."

Oh'Dar thought for a moment. "I can't do as you ask; I'm sorry. It does not matter where they are. They're safe and healthy," he said. "You must trust me, Mr. Storis. The sheriff told me you weren't just a business acquaintance—that you had a personal relationship with them. I believe you're here out of concern for their welfare, but I assure you they're not in any trouble. For personal reasons, they decided to leave behind their life at Shadow Ridge. Please respect their wishes."

As Honovi translated, she and Chief Is'Taqa exchanged glances.

Just then, there was a commotion outside. Pajackok was riding into the village leading a horse with a scuffed up Waschini rider mounted atop. The brave dismounted and gestured that the other should also get down. Tucker slid off his mount, and Pajackok handed the reins to one of the braves and asked him to take care of it.

"What kind of man treats an animal like this?" Pajackok said in Tucker's face, motioning wildly, even as he knew that the Waschini could not understand a word. Then he spat on the ground just in front of Tucker's feet. Turning to the crowd that had gathered, he explained. "I found him trying to sneak up on us. Only he was so noisy and smells so bad that he could never have gotten away with it."

Storis left the shelter and stomped over to Tucker, "What are you doing here? I told you to stay put!"

Tucker ignored Storis and turned to Oh'Dar. "So, you must be that Morgan kid everyone was looking for about twenty-five years ago? Seems to me they searched this here village back then. If the law finds out they were hiding you, then it could go hard for your friends here—even after all this time. Why, they might even be driven off and their land taken as punishment."

Oh'Dar frowned and stole a glance at Honovi and the Chief. She had been quietly translating the conversation.

"There's nothing more to be done here." Oh'Dar looked at Storis and shot an icy glare at the other man. "I suggest you stay another night, allow your horses to rest and be properly fed, and then go on your way. I promise you, Storis, my grandparents are not in any danger."

Storis frowned and shook his head. "Why should I believe you? Maybe you're just like your uncle Louis. What if you faked their deaths to get to their money!"

"That's preposterous, and you know it!" said

Oh'Dar. "You drew up the papers to leave Shadow Ridge and a fortune to Mrs. Thomas!"

"Yes, but that was just a portion of it. What about the rest? No, this isn't over, Morgan. I'll get to the bottom of this somehow."

Then the lawyer turned to Chief Is'Taqa. "Thank you for your hospitality. We will leave in the morning, but first, I will uncover the truth."

Pajackok gladly escorted both Waschini back to Storis' shelter.

Oh'Dar turned to Chief Is'Taqa and Honovi. "I do not know what to do. Should I have gone and fetched my grandparents? If he only wants to know they are alright, perhaps I should have appeased him." He ran a hand over his face.

"It is difficult to know which is best," said Chief Is'Taqa. "It is possible that if this man could speak with them and see they are healthy and content, that it would be the end of it. For the other Waschini, though, I do not know."

Oh'Dar shook his head. "I have brought trouble to us. Here. To our home. You have done nothing but care for me and help raise me, and I have repaid you with this. I must go and talk to Storis. It is a difficult trip for my grandparents, but the less information I give, the more it will pique curiosity."

"Perhaps the man would be satisfied with speaking to one of them," Chief Is'Taqa suggested.

Oh'Dar nodded and left for the men's shelter.

He pulled open the flap and stepped inside. Ignoring Tucker, he spoke directly to the lawyer.

"If you can speak with Ben Jenkins, would that convince you they're happy and well?" Oh'Dar asked.

Storis got to his feet. "Why not both of them?"

"You've traveled this area. You know it's a difficult journey. I wish to spare my grandmother the hardship," Oh'Dar explained.

Storis thought for a moment, "I don't mean to cause trouble. I only want to know they aren't being held somewhere against their will. So yes, if I can speak with Ben, I'll accept this was their decision, and they weren't coerced. But I'm warning you, I'll know if you're forcing him to lie."

"I'll be back sometime tomorrow," said Oh'Dar, still ignoring Tucker. "We agree then, that after you speak with Ben, you'll leave and not look back. You'll leave them to the life they have chosen?"

"Yes."

It was mid-morning by the time Oh'Dar returned with Ben. As they entered the village, he spotted Storis and Tucker sitting at a fire, eating.

Out of the corner of his eye, Storis saw them coming. He set down his meal and jumped to his feet.

"Ben Jenkins," he said, grabbing the older man's hand.

"Newell," said Ben. "Grayson explained to me why you're here. I'm sorry for the ruse. Come, walk with us." The three men stepped away, out of earshot of Tucker.

Tucker also stood up, but Pajackok stepped in front of him and glared until the tracker sat back down.

"What's this all about, Ben?" asked Storis.

"We're both fine. This is what we wanted. And I'm sorry you had to be put through believing we'd died. But it was the only way to prevent—just this. Well-meaning people following us and not giving us the privacy to make our own choices."

"You could simply have said you were leaving Shadow Ridge," Storis objected as they walked together.

"I'm sorry, but you're proof we couldn't. People are curious about anything that smacks of mystery, and we wanted to put an end to any ideas of revenge that Louis might have had," Ben explained. "I hear he was arrested at the funeral, but he might not have been. Again, this was the best way for all involved."

He stopped and turned to face the lawyer. "And so my question now is, will you let it go? Will you accept that Vivian and I are happy? That we chose this to be close to our grandson and his new wife. You're still young enough, Newell. In time you'll understand the importance of family. Of feeling that you're a part of something bigger than yourself."

Ben put his hand on Storis' shoulder, "Now, who is that rough-looking fellow with you?"

Storis let out a long sigh. "I hired him to follow young Mr. Morgan. When I learned from the Webbs that you were still alive and that Mr. Morgan was coming back for supplies, I hired Tucker to follow him. Then, I paid him to bring me here, to find you."

"Grayson explained a lot of this to me on the way here. I believe, though, that he threatened to bring trouble to these people here, after all these years," said Ben.

"He's a sly one, always looking for an angle. But I can handle him. Is there anything I can do for you and Miss Vivian?"

"Just respect our privacy. How is Mrs. Thomas doing?" Ben asked. "How are things in Millgrove?"

"Mrs. Thomas is doing very well; her son and his family have moved into Shadow Ridge. As far as Millgrove goes, it isn't the same without you and Miss Vivian. My business has pretty much dried up. I am thinking of moving to Wilde Edge."

"That's the Webbs' little town," said Oh'Dar, absentmindedly.

"They don't have a lawyer. Found that out when I was dealing with the banker over the Webbs' mortgaged land. And the Webbs were very kind to me. Perhaps, in a way, being around them makes me still feel a bit connected to the Morgans," he added, very honestly.

Oh'Dar looked at the lawyer and felt a pang.

Perhaps I've misjudged him. He seems sincere, and he does seem to care about my grandparents.

"So, you're living somewhere else? With another tribe then?" asked Storis.

Ben pursed his lips, "I will tell you that we're healthy and happy and cared for. And that's where it has to end. We've trusted each other since we first met. Please trust me again and allow us our privacy." He searched the lawyer's face.

"I will," said Storis. "I'll collect Tucker, and we'll be on our way."

⁂

When they were ready to leave, Storis extended his hand to Oh'Dar and said, "If there's ever anything I can help you with, please, find a way to get in touch with me at Wilde Edge. I'll be moving there directly."

"Well, yes, you might be able to help me," said Oh'Dar. "Also, when you do get settled in Wilde Edge, please contact the banker there and let him know we're connected. It might come in handy someday for you to have an established business association."

Ben and Oh'Dar watched while the men mounted their horses and were led away by Pajackok and a few other braves.

"Do you think he's satisfied with having seen Ben?" asked Honovi, walking up to them.

"I hope so," said Oh'Dar. "I certainly hope so."

Before turning back to the village, Pajackok and the other braves kept a careful eye on the two forms until they were well out of sight.

*

"So, you got what you wanted. And I expect you to pay me that extra when we return to Wilde Edge," said Tucker.

"You'll get your money, don't worry. But after that's settled, I expect us never to speak again," Storis said, eyes straight ahead.

"I've served my purpose then? Is that it?" Tucker taunted him.

"Something like that. Look, there's no reason for us to quarrel. Other than not staying away from the village as I told you, you did your part."

"You're moving to Wilde Edge then?"

"Yes. And once we get back, we'll go our separate ways and speak no more of this. Whatever business we had is completed, and the matter is over and settled as far as I'm concerned," Storis answered.

If it's so settled, then why do you keep sneaking away and making that little map of yours, thought Tucker. *And it may be over and settled as far as you're concerned, but it sure as hell isn't as far as I'm concerned.*

CHAPTER 13

Everything was as ready as could be. Excitement was running high in anticipation of the visitors. At mealtimes, the People would be mingling with the Leaders and other guests from the other communities. Often these visitors carried news of loved ones who had been paired to members of those communities, or for some other reason, had relocated, and socializing was a special event in itself. But in addition to the usual excitement, unlike other gatherings, this time the community would be allowed to hear some of the High Council proceedings.

The first to arrive were Chief Is'Taqa, Honovi, and Ithua, who was still the senior Medicine Woman. Acaraho and Adia were at the entrance, waiting to greet them. At their side stood Nootau, heir to the leadership of the High Rocks. Adia warmly wrapped her arms around Ithua in greeting.

Chief Is'Taqa and Honovi stayed with the group at the front to greet the Chiefs of the other villages. A feeling of respect and reverence hung in the air as they waited for their honored guests to arrive.

Second to reach Kthama was Chief Cha'Tima from a village south of the Little River. It was a high tribute to the importance of the event that the Chief and his companions would travel so far. Then arrived Risik'Tar, his mate, Icider, and his Healer Tapia, followed by Harak'Sar with his mate, Habil, and lastly, Urilla Wuti and Iella. Iella quickly stole a glance at her beloved Nootau as they walked past. Adia's eyes filled with tears of joy at again seeing her friend Urilla Wuti.

Slowly everyone filed in, and as each arrived, Mapiya and other females were waiting to show them to their quarters and tend to any needs. Older offspring had been recruited as runners to help carry messages. Those chosen took their role seriously and treated everyone with the utmost respect and courtesy.

The rest would trickle in over the next two days. If everyone arrived as planned, the first assembly would take place in two mornings' time. That left some space for acquaintances and friendships to be renewed before the official program started.

When her formal greeting duties were over for the day, Adia immediately sought out Urilla Wuti. As soon as she was given permission to enter, she pulled open the wooden door and ran over to hug the older Healer.

"I have missed you so!" Urilla Wuti exclaimed.

"And I have missed you! I am so glad you came; we have a great deal to catch up on." Adia disengaged herself and turned to hug Iella, who was sitting across the room.

"Where is An'Kru?" Iella asked.

"Nadiwani is watching him at the moment."

"I was helping Urilla Wuti get settled; now that you are here, I will go and find your son!" And Iella left with a smile.

After Iella had gone, Adia looked Urilla Wuti over, head to toe. "You look well. I am pleased."

"Oddly enough, being Overseer does not take up as much time as I had thought," she chuckled. "But I can sense you are troubled. What is it, my dear friend?"

"Just struggling with the unknown. Haan told us that the six female Guardians are seeded. And that An'Kru must never be in the presence of the twelve until *the appointed time*. There is so much mystery. So much I do not know even about my own son, An'Kru. What is his purpose here? I do not like feeling anxious, but despite Pan's reassurances, I cannot seem to shake it."

"Pan!" Urilla Wuti exclaimed. "Is she here?"

"No, I met her in the Corridor. She told me that all is as it should be with An'Kru. Perhaps it is time we reach out to E'ranale while Nadiwani is watching him."

Before long, Urilla Wuti and Adia were once more in the Corridor, in the beautiful garden with the hills and rocks of Kthama far in the background. They took in every blissful second of being there.

They were soon joined by E'ranale, who smiled warmly at them both. "I am glad you came. It is time for you to learn about the nature of evil," she said. "To understand evil, you must first understand the nature of good. There is but one infinite power, and it is only benevolent, loving, kind. And because of that, the life force it emanates can only be positive. And positivity is pleasure; no matter whether it is the pleasure of peace, comfort, rest after a long day, the enjoyment of the beauty of creation, the deep soul-satisfaction of helping others, love. Everything that comes from the One-Who-Is-Three can only be good. So then, where does evil come from?"

E'ranale stopped to make sure the Healers understood her so far. "I have spoken to you of the life force entering your realm and how it can become distorted. And because, at its core, the life force is pleasure itself, when the life current becomes distorted, pleasure does too. It becomes twisted. Dark. And this twisted pleasure is the source of evil. It is pleasure derived from the suffering of others.

Hatred, cruelty, revenge; all have a pleasurable element to them. There is a cathartic release in unleashing one's anger. Very few will admit to this; however, it is true. As another example, jealousy feels satisfaction when the object of that jealousy suffers a setback or loses something of value. Punishment, revenge, knowingly causing harm to another —whether physical or otherwise—are all examples of this twisted, destructive pleasure."

"But what of justice? Is it also evil to long for justice?" asked Adia.

"Justice is not revenge. It is in our nature, our soul's nature, to long for justice. Any responsible family or society must have restrictions and boundaries for behavior. Righting and limiting wrongs, addressing the bad acts of others is not evil. It starts down the path to evil only when we take a sinister pleasure in another's suffering when they are corrected or their behavior is curtailed. There are many steps between experiencing a momentary dark pleasure to nurturing it and entering a true state of evil. Do you understand?" E'ranale asked.

Both Healers nodded.

"Remember I said that there is only one power, and it is positive. So evil can only take the positivity and distort it. It has no power separate from the life current itself. The irony is that evil is in itself still seeking pleasure, which is the true nature of the life force—only its means of achieving pleasure have become distorted. And because we are created to be social beings, evil has a way of finding other evil with which to join up. With no dissenting voice to show them their error, their distortion is reinforced and augmented by collective agreement, even though that is usually unspoken."

"Are you speaking of the Hue'Mahns?" asked Adia.

"My daughter has explained to you that the Waschini's distorted approach is not confined to them. But, at present, they represent the largest volume of it, and it is spreading among them. However, there is another element at play here. It is not just the Hue'Mahns. It is even more powerful than the Waschini and the others of the Hue'Mahns who are out of alignment with creation."

Adia and Urilla Wuti waited, their eyes locked on E'ranale's.

"A long time ago, at the time of the great division between those who followed my mate Moc'Tor, and his brother Straf'Tor, there was another split within the population that had followed Straf'Tor to Kayerm. It was a time of great transition and strife, and conflict arose. As a result of the trouble they caused, a rebel group of Mothoc was expelled from Straf'Tor's community. Since their alienation from the others, they have lived in isolation, becoming more and more bitter and resentful of the Akassa and the Sarnonn. As the Aezaiterian flow comes most strongly through the Mothoc, their distortion of the creative force is very powerful. On their own, it would take centuries for the negativity of the Hue'Mahns to cause total devastation to Etera. But with the powerful Mothoc contributing to it, it is gaining strength more quickly."

"Can these Mothoc be stopped? Destroyed?" asked Adia.

"No. Etera needs them. Etera needs all the ancient Mothoc in existence, even if some of them have lost their way. Though the Sarnonn channel the Aezaiterian force into Etera, they are not as powerful as the Mothoc."

"But did you not say," Urilla Wuti interjected, "that a Guardian is able to cleanse negativity from the life force?"

"Yes," said E'ranale. "And the newly created Sarnonn Guardians have a part to play."

Adia said quietly, "So does An'Kru."

E'ranale looked at her, and Adia felt a rush of love sweeping through her being.

"Yes. So does An'Kru. For now, the balance is holding, but in time there will be a battle. And the roles of both your sons will be critical, as will the role of another. Because an individual who turns away from evil can become an even greater force for good than one who has never fallen away."

Adia thought of Khon'Tor.

"Yes, Khon'Tor. He is an example of this. As you have accepted, his transformation is pure. His soul is very powerful now—more than it ever was when he was the Leader of the High Rocks—but his self-hatred blocks his ability to see his own worth."

Adia looked down, seemingly lost in thought.

"We are still waiting for Pan to appear," said Urilla Wuti.

"My daughter will make her appearance soon. It is she who must train the six male Guardians and An'Kru to use their powers as Guardians of Etera.

"Now, it is time for you to return to your realm. I have given you much to assimilate."

And with that, Adia and Urilla Wuti suddenly found themselves back on the sleeping mats in Urilla Wuti's room.

"I am exhausted," the older Healer said, turning her head toward Adia.

"So am I. Oh, but Urilla," she exclaimed. "An'Kru must take part in a battle? And Nootau as well? I cannot think but that both their lives could be at risk. How am I to make peace with this?"

Urilla Wuti reached out and squeezed Adia's hand. Not really expecting an answer, Adia squeezed her hand back and sat up. "You get some rest; I must go find An'Kru and hold him in my arms."

Urilla Wuti nodded and let exhaustion carry her into sleep, but not before beseeching the Great Mother to protect Adia and her family.

Adia cuddled An'Kru and let him nurse. As she watched him, she felt anxiety fill her. *What is to be your destiny? Whatever it is, I must not let fear drive my decisions.*

After holding him for some time, Adia put her offspring in his little nest and surrendered herself to sleep.

She woke to find herself in the Great Chamber and took a moment to get her bearings before looking around. It was deserted except for one figure standing in the shadows. She started to approach, and it stepped out toward her.

"Nootau. What are you doing here?" *What am I doing here?*

"Mama. I do not know. I lay down to sleep, and then all of a sudden, I was here."

Adia reached out to take her son's hand. It felt as real as ever. "You do not remember coming here?" she asked, squeezing his fingers.

"No," he answered.

Neither do I. "At the Far High Hills, you have continued working with Urilla Wuti, have you not?"

"Yes," responded Nootau. "But nothing like this has ever happened. Are you saying this is not real? That we are not actually talking in the Great Chamber? How can that be? I can feel the rock floor under my feet. I can feel your hand holding mine. I can even smell your familiar scent."

"I am certain I know what has happened. We are in what is called the Dream World. Has Urilla Wuti been working with you on how to enter this realm?" *I do not remember Urilla Wuti ever mentioning entering the Dream World. Has she somehow discovered it and been teaching Nootau?*

"No, she has not told me anything of this," answered Nootau. "What is it—and how do you know of it?"

"Your father and I met here before we were paired."

"Here? How often? Why?" he asked.

Adia felt her cheeks burning, "Why does not matter. But it is surprising to me that on your own, you have somehow learned how to enter the Dream World."

"Are you saying I am really sleeping next to Iella in our room? Then I do not understand how everything here can feel so real."

"Yes. Your body is back in your quarters. Our consciousness—who we are—is not tied to the life of our bodies; it exists outside of them. Our bodies are just shells that we inhabit here in Etera's realm."

Nootau ran his hand over the top of one of the long stone slabs that made up the tables. "It feels the same. I do not know what to say."

"I have no idea if this is tied to your ability to hear information, as you told me happened during the attack by the Sarius Snake. You are gifted, Nootau; let us see where this goes. And we must tell Urilla Wuti. I had to work with her for some time before I could enter the Dream World."

Nootau nodded, "Of course. So, how do we get back?"

"Just will yourself to wake up. You can leave any time. I am curious, though, to see if, having experienced the Dream World now, you can will yourself to enter it. Shall we try to meet here again tomorrow night? As an experiment?" she asked.

"Yes, Mama." And Nootau gave his mother a huge hug. "I would never have believed this if I had not experienced it. I could not have imagined this was possible."

Nootau's eyes snapped open, and he found he was back in his body, lying next to his sleeping mate.

The next morning, Adia hastened to find Urilla Wuti to tell her what had happened. "You mentioned that the Corridor might be the answer to your vision of Healers being able to communicate across long distances. But could the Dream World also be an option?" Adia asked.

Urilla Wuti was stirring her tea with a long and beautiful crystal.

"Where did you find that?" Adia asked. "It is lovely!"

"Your son gave this to me. Nootau. When he and Iella were looking for fluorite some way north of the Far High Hills, they found a series of caves with a whole crop of these. And it is so much prettier than using my finger!" Urilla Wuti tapped it on the side of the gourd and laid it on the table.

Adia felt a twinge of jealousy that Nootau had given Urilla Wuti such a gift.

"It also feels pleasant to hold. So many of the rocks do, do they not?"

"Yes," Adia replied. "As if they have an energy of their own." Her thoughts went back to what E'ranale had said about all creation having life force within—even inanimate objects. She also remembered the granite boulders that had transformed into giant crystals when the twelve Sarnonn Guardians were formed.

"Back to the Dream World," said Urilla Wuti. "Let us explore this with the other Healers when we meet separately from the High Council."

It was time. Adia, Nadiwani, and the other Circle of Counsel members sat toward the front of the Great Chamber.

Acaraho strode in, the 'Tor Leader's Staff in his hand. All eyes turned to watch him while others scanned the room, no doubt looking for Khon'Tor.

The new Leader waited a moment before raising the staff overhead. "Greetings and welcome, every-one. No doubt those who have not heard are wondering why I stand before you, holding the 'Tor Leader's Staff in place of Khon'Tor. Much has happened since we last met, and you will be hearing about it over the next few days. Khon'Tor has relinquished the leadership of the People of the High Rocks to me. He and his mate Tehya now reside at the Far High Hills, where Tehya's family lives. Rest assured, however; we will not go without the benefit of Khon'Tor's wisdom as he will continue to take part in the High Council meetings.

"As you look around, you will have noticed that we have many guests in our midst. The High Council has been expanded to include Healers and Healer Helpers, and we have called the full High Council, which means our Brothers' Leaders are also with us. Acaraho then explained that Urilla Wuti was now the Overseer and told them of the passing of the great beloved Chief Ogima.

Everyone sat transfixed as he went on to explain what had been learned over the past few years about their true history—a history involving the Mothoc, the Sarnonn, the People, and the Brothers. Acaraho told them about the discovery and opening of Kthama Minor. He told them of the Wall of Records that held the accounting of the Age of Darkness. Then he asked Adia to come forward and share her knowledge.

She spoke of the creative life force that permeated every bit of creation. She explained the concept of the Hue'Mahns and the unity they all shared, and the threat brought to Etera by negative consciousness. She revealed that they now realized the Brothers, the Sarnonn, and the People were all related to some extent. Half the day passed before enough had been shared.

The room was completely silent throughout.

When they had both finished, Acaraho said, "No doubt all we have shared has given you a great deal to think about, as it has us—though we have had time to make peace with it. But now, I ask Haan, Adik'Tar of the Sarnonn, who are now our neighbors, to come forward."

Motion in the back of the room caused all heads to turn. An audible gasp rose from the visitors as the giant figure of Haan stepped out from the shadows and walked to Acaraho's side.

Haan looked over the crowd before saying, "I stand here as your protector, just as the Fathers-Of-Us-All were before us. My people and I are pledged to help you. You need have no fear of us." Then he looked directly from one Chief to the next, "For the sins of our fathers against your people, I bring you our deepest apologies."

The Chiefs glanced at each other, leaned over, murmured. Some shook their heads, while others bowed theirs in silence.

Haan continued with how the ancient Mothoc had interbred with the Brothers Without Their Consent, and how the Sarnonn and Akassa were created as a result. He explained they did not know how it was accomplished, only that the Sarnonn and the Akassa were proof that it took place. He shared his and his people's deep shame in what was done, and when he had finished, asked for their forgiveness.

Silence filled the Great Chamber.

Acaraho broke the silence, "These next few days will awaken you to new truths. Truths which will challenge many of your long-held beliefs, just as they have ours. One of those beliefs is about the nature of the Waschini. As I look out over the crowd, I see the faces of most of those who would have been at the High Council meeting decades ago, when the threat of the Waschini was first discussed. A threat that was believed would usher in the Wrak-Wavara, The Age of Shadows. We have learned so much since then, as you have already heard shared by others here today."

Acaraho walked over to the other side of the stage. "No doubt everyone knows the story of the Waschini child adopted by Adia, Healer of the High Rocks. That offspring has grown to adulthood and found his place here among our people and among the Brothers. He has recently been paired with the daughter of Chief Is'Taqa. Through Oh'Dar, we have learned that our beliefs about the Waschini were clouded by prejudice and selective reports of their cruelty. While there is an element of evil in all of us, and perhaps the Waschini are at the forefront of the problems facing Etera, to condemn an entire species because of the acts of a few is wrong. Over the years, Oh'Dar has learned about his Waschini blood-family. And we have also learned. I wish now to introduce you to Oh'Dar, and to his Waschini grand-parents who have come to live with us at Kthama."

Acaraho motioned toward the back of the room, and all heads turned to see Oh'Dar enter with Miss Vivian and Ben.

The three walked slowly to the front, Miss Vivian tightly holding Ben's hand. They turned to face the crowd, and Oh'Dar spoke. "These are my grandpar-ents, Miss Vivian and Ben. They have left the Waschini world behind to live among us. They have much to learn about our way of life, but they also have much to teach us. Please welcome them. Please understand they come in peace and wish only to join us in creating the future of our own making."

Adia looked at Urilla Wuti, knowing they were both praying the crowd would accept Oh'Dar's grandparents, or if they did not, at least would hold their silence about it.

After a respectful moment, Acaraho said, "Much has been shared on which you no doubt need time to reflect. And there is much more to come over the next few days. Let us adjourn for midday meal. Then there will be a meeting of the High Council, and afterward, we will all gather again at evening meal. If any of you wish to discuss these matters further, Mapiya or High Protector Awan will find you a place to do so."

Acaraho struck his Leader's Staff onto the floor, and everyone started to disperse.

Oh'Dar led his grandparents to the side of the

room. "Oh Grayson—Oh'Dar," Miss Vivian said. "This is like a fairy tale. Some fantastical story. Surely this can't be happening—and yet it is. No matter how difficult, how different this life is, I'm so glad we came with you."

Oh'Dar leaned over and hugged his grandmother as Ben patted him on the shoulder. Slowly, a small group of well-wishers joined them, and Oh'Dar translated their welcoming comments.

As the crowd started to disperse, from his place at the front, Acaraho could see Larara, Kurak'Kahn's mate, in the crowd. On the other side of the room, he noticed Kurak'Kahn himself. He knew of Larara's matter with the High Council, but he was unsure of the reason for her mate's presence.

With the midday meal over, the High Council members had assembled. With the attendance of the Brothers' Chiefs, the Healers and Helpers, and Haan and his people, they'd had to find a far larger private room than they had used before. Haan stood at the back, easily seeing over the heads of those seated in front of him. At his side stood Qirrik, his High Protector, and next to him, the Healer, Artadel. Though she was his Third Rank, Haaka had elected to stay behind with Kalli.

Once settled, Urilla Wuti opened the meeting,

first asking for business from any visitors petitioning the High Council.

Larara, sitting in the back, quietly stood. She looked around the room, spotted her mate, and glanced back at the new Overseer.

"I come to petition for Bak'tah-Awhidi from Kurak'Kahn, my mate." She looked around nervously.

"Kurak'Kahn," said the new Overseer. "Your mate has asked for Bak'tah-Awhidi. Since you are here, I must ask if you object."

Kurak'Kahn rose, "I do not object. Please grant her freedom." Then he sat as quietly as he had stood.

"Since there is no objection, you do not need to provide cause," said Urilla Wuti. "Your pairing is hereby dissolved. You are both free to search for happiness on another path."

"Please," Larara said, "I have another request." Then, in the silence that followed, she continued. "I wish to ask the help of the other communities, including those of the Brothers. My niece, Linoi, bore a son. Out of avarice, her mate took the offspring. We do not know where our great-nephew is. Our niece is dead. Whether by the act of another's hand or her own, or by accident, we do not know. Nothing can relieve the heartache of her loss, but if the offspring could be recovered, it would ease some of our suffering. Please." Then she turned to Khon'-Tor, "I am thankful to you, Khon'Tor, for your efforts to find the offspring." Then she looked back at the crowd, "Though U'Kail has not been found, Khon'Tor did find proof that my daughter's mate perished.

"Please be mindful of this tragedy, and should there be any sign of U'Kail, please send word. Perhaps, by some miracle, he was not murdered by my daughter's mate. Perhaps he is safe somewhere, rescued by someone who does not know where he belongs." Then Larara put her hands to her face to cover her tears.

Adia went across and put an arm around Larara, who leaned for a moment against the Healer's shoulder. Then Larara straightened up, thanked Adia, and made her way to the back of the room. High Protector Awan opened the door and then silently closed it behind her.

"Anyone else?" Urilla Wuti asked quietly.

Kurak'Kahn stood. "There are limits to how much heartache one can bear. My presence is only adding to Larara's pain and suffering. I, therefore, ask for acceptance into another community."

"Who here will open their community to Kurak'Kahn?" asked Urilla Wuti.

After a moment, Gatin'Rar of the Little River stood, "You are welcome at our community."

Kurak'Kahn thanked him. "I have everything with me that I wish to take. If you are agreeable, I will travel with you when you leave." Then, one last time, he regarded those watching him, many of whom he had once led in his position of Overseer.

He purposefully kept his eyes averted from Khon'Tor and Acaraho before finally leaving the room.

With the private matters resolved, Urilla Wuti asked the Brothers' Chiefs to share on behalf of their villages.

One by one, the Chiefs stood up. One after another, they spoke of trouble brewing with the Waschini. Tales of intimidation, riders coming close and circling the villages. Some altercations in which the Waschini had engaged outright with their braves. Tales of formidable weapons brandished about, of women and children terrorized by the intruders. Everyone listened reverently, with heavy hearts.

As their stories came to an end, Urilla Wuti spoke. "We are all saddened by this news. We feared there would eventually be a threat from the Waschini, but we did not know it had progressed so far. The People's existence is hidden from their knowledge, but we might well wonder for how long. We must pray together, now, for your protection and welfare. And for guidance from the Great Spirit."

The room became silent as each heart and soul reached out in their own way, beseeching the One-Who-is-Three, the Great Spirit, for answers.

Urilla Wuti opened her eyes and looked across the room, waiting for the others to raise their heads. Finally, she spoke, "We will adjourn now as it is nearing evening meal. Please relax and enjoy yourselves. Healers and Healer Helpers, after we have eaten, we will meet alone here. Thank you."

Oh'Dar was sitting with his grandparents and Nootau when the High Council members returned. Soon his parents, Nadiwani, and Iella joined them.

"Have you eaten?" asked Adia.

"Yes, just finished," said Oh'Dar. "How was the meeting?"

"Some general business," said Acaraho. "Then the Chiefs shared. Every one of them reported trouble from the Waschini. Even threats of being driven from their homes. Threats of taking the land of their livelihoods."

Oh'Dar thought back to the threat made by the man, Tucker. "The Waschini believe they can own the land. Just as my grandparents owned thousands of acres at what they call Shadow Ridge."

"How is that possible?" Nadiwani asked.

"It is a concept, a thought, that they made into an agreement—like a law. They claim portions of the land as their own. Much like we and the Brothers accept and respect the boundaries of our own territories."

"It feels different," said Adia.

"It is different. Because we are willing to honor the fact that certain areas are used by the Brothers, and certain areas are used by the People. The Waschini go a step further and draw up a written agreement, and put a value on the land they then *own*."

"How can you put a value on land? It is a gift of the Great Spirit, along with everything else on Etera," Adia said. "I find this difficult to grasp."

"Once someone *owns* that area of land, they believe they have the right to control who comes onto it, who gets to hunt on it and otherwise use its resources," he explained.

"So the Waschini seek to drive the Brothers from their homes in an effort to take over the areas they inhabit?" clarified Acaraho.

"What can we do to help the Brothers?" asked Adia.

"I cannot think of anything we can do," said Acaraho. "The Waschini must never know of our existence, and that ties our hands." Then he added, "And the same is true of the Sarnonn."

Urilla Wuti approached the table, and they made room for her next to Adia.

When they had finished eating, Urilla Wuti suggested that she, Adia, Iella, and Nadiwani return to the meeting room. She started to lead them away but then returned to the table. "Nootau. Come with us."

⚘

Once everyone was seated, Urilla Wuti explained why she had asked them to meet collectively. It took quite a while to fill everyone in on how, for years, she and Adia had been working together to enhance their abilities. She told them about the Ror'Eckrah, the One-Mind to which the Sarnonn connected to open Kthama Minor, and the release of energy that had followed.

Adia shared how her own abilities had become augmented since that time. She wove it into the story of the Wall of Records and the transformation of the twelve Sarnonn into Guardians.

Urilla Wuti then asked Iella and Nootau to step forward. She introduced them and told the group about Iella's new-found ability to communicate with animals. She explained that Nootau seemed to pick up messages, though, at present, these messages came only at their own bidding. Then she asked if any of them had noticed anything peculiar themselves.

Though none of them shared anything specific, all agreed that their abilities also seemed to be growing stronger.

Finally, Urilla Wuti closed by sharing her vision of communicating across distances and her work to that end. She had intended to speak of the Corridor but instead spoke of the Dream World.

"While you are here, Adia and I want to work individually with any of you who feel drawn to this idea. We hope that when you leave, you will practice what we show you and continue to develop your ability to enter the Dream World."

Just as Urilla Wuti finished, one of the Healers spoke up. "Excuse me, please, but the male you introduced who is paired to your niece—is he a male Healer? If so, that is unheard of."

Adia stepped forward to answer, explaining how they had learned from the Wall of Records that Healers used to be male or female. And that while Nootau was not a Healer specifically, he was showing signs of supernatural abilities. "Nootau has himself recently visited the Dream World."

There was a murmuring of excited chatter.

Then another female slowly stood up. "Please forgive me, Healer Adia, but we have heard talk of your new son. Will we be given the honor of seeing him before we leave Kthama? Is he— We were told he is some type of Guardian. One of those who have the power to protect Etera."

Adia sighed, any idea of shielding her son from the limelight vanishing. She nodded, "Yes. If you wish, I will bring him to the general meeting on the last day."

"What of the adult Guardians? Will we get to meet them?"

"There is much to cover in only a few days," said Adia. "But I have no doubt you will all meet some of the Guardians before we part."

"Only some of them? But we heard that there are twelve," another Healer said.

"An'Kru cannot be in the presence of the twelve Guardians until an appointed time," Adia shared. "Great care must be taken to keep them from proximity to each other."

"Why? What will happen?" someone asked.

"I do not know," answered Adia. "We are only given bits and pieces of information over time."

Eyes widened as the mystery enchanted them all.

"We are blessed to be living in such mystical times," a Healer Helper shared, and nods passed through the gathering.

Adia was doing her best to welcome the interest in her son, but inside she was struggling. *I do not want to share An'Kru with everyone. How can I protect him if he is the constant focus of attention wherever I take him? How will he ever grow up to be normal? But that is just it—he is not normal, and he never will be. And why does Haan not come forward and freely tell us all he knows? And where is Pan?*

She stopped ruminating because she could feel Urilla Wuti watching her.

"It has been a long day," the older Healer said. "Tomorrow has been set aside for socializing and any other business to which we need to attend. During the day, therefore, Adia and I will work with those of you who are interested in learning how to enter the Dream World."

When the others had left, Urilla Wuti spoke to Adia. "You must take some time tomorrow to be by yourself. Promise me you will."

Adia sat down and slumped over, holding her head in her hands. "I cannot make peace with this. I cannot make peace with an unknown future for Nootau and An'Kru. Now *both* of them are to be caught up in this! And these other feelings I am having—jealousy for one. Jealousy that Nootau now confides in you. Petty jealousy that he gave you that beautiful fluorite crystal. I do not want to be like this!"

Urilla Wuti sat down next to her and took Adia's hands in hers. "Look at me. Look at me," she repeated, and Adia lifted her gaze.

"You have been brought through everything so far. There is no reason to believe you would be abandoned now or that you will lose all you hold most dear. You cannot live in fear; however you do it, you must reconnect with your faith that things are unfolding as they should."

"Why does Haan not tell us everything he knows? It seems we only get a piece here and a piece there. How can I not fear that next he will reveal something terrible about An'Kru's future?"

"I cannot answer that; perhaps Haan is the only one who can," Urilla Wuti suggested quietly.

The next morning, Adia woke to find Acaraho already gone. She was grateful he had let her sleep but now urgently wanted to find him before he became embroiled in the day's activities.

She gathered her food selections and sat at the usual table. For a while, she listened to the idle chatter of her family, but it did not distract her from her worries.

"You were asleep when I came in last night, Saraste'" Acaraho said to her. "And sound asleep this morning when I left. You seem unusually tired of late."

Adia looked away, trying to hide her emotions.

"What is it, Mama?" Nootau asked. "You are filled with worry."

Adia looked at those seated with her. *My family. I always feel I have to be so strong. But if I can never lean on them, then I am truly alone.*

"It is many things. I cannot shake the feelings that seem to dominate me now. Fear. Anxiety. Doubt."

"You are worried about An'Kru," Nootau said.

Adia nodded. "And about you," she admitted.

"Then let my faith shore you up, Mama. I am not afraid of what is to come. Whatever it is, we will handle it together," Nootau continued. "Just as we have everything else."

"I have so many unanswered questions," she said. "And Haan never gives enough information to understand the whole story. Why is he not telling us all of what he knows?"

Nootau looked off across the room. Finally, he said, "Haan cannot." He brought his gaze back to his mother. "He cannot. Because he does not know any more than what he shares at the time. These are coded memories, deeply embedded in some type of ancient memory. He does not know the information until it surfaces. Until something triggers it and a certain amount of information is suddenly available to him."

Adia stared at her son.

"How do you know this?" Acaraho asked.

"The same way I know the other information that has been given to me; I hear it in my mind. Perhaps the same way it is for Haan," Nootau suggested. "He is not withholding information from you, Mama. He simply does not know it until he knows it. He cannot will it to appear."

Urilla Wuti and Adia exchanged glances.

"Thank you, son," said Acaraho.

"Do you feel better now?" Iella asked Adia. "It seems like you do, somewhat."

"Yes, that helped a lot; thank you Nootau," Feeling some of her faith return, Adia reached across the table and touched her son's arm. *Haan is not withholding what he knows. It is given to him at the appointed time. There is a stronger power behind that which we can see.*

CHAPTER 14

I t was the last day. All the matters before the High Council had been settled. The Leaders had met to talk about the bloodline challenges that faced all their communities. They had also been given ample time to meet in small groups and to mingle with the others at the High Rocks, inhabitants and visitors alike.

Urilla Wuti and Adia had met with some of the other Healers and started work with them. The two made sure each had the knowledge to practice alone once they returned to their own communities.

Khon'Tor had been involved in all the Leader meetings. It had been worthwhile coming, yet he did not understand why it was so crucial for him to have been there. He was relieved the last day had come; like it or not, he was returning to Tehya and Arismae at the Far High Hills. He often wondered if Nootau had talked to Acaraho yet about who had truly seeded him.

Once they were all in place in the Great Chamber, Chief Cha'Tima stood and asked to address the crowd. With Acaraho's approval, he walked to the front of the room. He asked for Haan to come forward and join him.

Chief Cha'Tima raised his own staff in the air and waved it back and forth before turning to face Haan. "Truth about the betrayal of our people long ago has been spoken by you, Haan, Leader of the Sarnonn, who now walk among us. We believed that the haired ones were long-gone from Etera—those who were once believed to be our protectors.

"The secret of this betrayal was known only to a few Chiefs. We have waited for generations for the sins against our ancestors to be acknowledged. And now, an apology has been offered. I and the other Chiefs assembled here have met long and privately about this matter. Before we adjourn, at the request of the Brothers' Chiefs, I accept the apology offered by the Sarnonn Leader on behalf of the Ancients. We are, after all, sons and daughters of the one Great Spirit. May there be only peace between all our peoples from now on and forever."

⁜

The assembly was about to adjourn. As promised, Adia had brought An'Kru to the Great Chamber.

Somehow, a line had formed of everyone who wanted to see the offspring, and she had stood with him in her arms as each person remarked at his striking looks before moving on. Finally, it seemed everyone had been given a chance to look at An'Kru, and she was relieved to wrap him up and remove him from the prying eyes.

Despite the curiosity over her son having been temporarily satisfied, Adia knew there was still something everyone was waiting for—the promised appearance of the six male Sarnonn Guardians who were scheduled to arrive at the end of the meeting.

Acaraho stood at the front, the Leader's staff in his hand. He thanked the visitors for coming and the People of the High Rocks for extending such hospitality. He promised the Brothers the unwavering support of the People and pledged that their peril at the hands of the Waschini would remain at the forefront of everyone's thoughts and prayers. He added that the People's Leaders were committed to help look for a solution.

Finally, it was time.

From the back, Haan entered with the six Guardians. Acaraho signaled for them to come forward, and as one, they moved to join him at the front.

The room was absolutely still as hundreds of eyes

silently took in the giants standing before them with their luxuriant white coats and their silver-grey eyes.

Haan introduced them, starting with Thord, the Leader of the Guardians. When all had been named, Thord stepped forward to speak.

The audience remained frozen.

"We cannot explain how we stand before you now, transformed in a way no one could have imagined. We know we possess powers, some we are aware of, and many we are not. But regardless of our abilities, they are meant for one purpose only. Service. Service to all who inhabit Etera, and service to Etera herself.

"We are on a journey together. We do not know the destination, only that it is for the good of all our communities. We do not know the path, only that our steps are ordered. We will learn and discover and grow together as we create the future of our own making."

Suddenly, a bright light burst out from the back of the room. Everyone gasped and quickly turned around.

As if materializing out of nowhere, stood a creature the likes of which had not been seen by any of the Brothers, People, or Sarnonn since the end of the previous age. It was taller even than the Sarnonn Guardians and bore a thick, silver-white coat that shimmered, though there was no other light falling on it. Deep-set silver-grey eyes seemed to see into each person's soul, and everything stopped. Every consciousness in the room was riveted on the figure standing before them.

Into everyone's mind, only one word appeared. Pan.

Adia stifled a gasp and unconsciously hugged An'Kru tighter. The real Pan. Then, to her shock, Pan walked over and reached for An'Kru.

Adia looked up, up into the silent grey eyes staring down at her. Her heart pounding in her chest, she clutched her son tighter. She found herself slowly shaking her head, *no*.

The Guardian gestured again, and Adia quieted her fears enough to realize that the grey eyes were filled with compassion and love. Tears rolling down her face, Adia slowly, carefully, held out An'Kru.

The words appeared in Adia's mind. "There is no truer trust than to surrender to another that which we would give our last breath to protect."

Carefully cradling the tiny bundle, Pan turned away from Adia and walked to the front of the room.

As she approached, Haan and the Sarnonn Guardians again fell to one knee. When they arose, each bumped a fist over his heart and bowed slightly before all said in unison, "An'Kru'Tor, The Promised One."

Pan turned to face the crowd, cradling An'Kru in her powerful yet gentle embrace. The offspring looked up at Pan and gurgled happily, reaching out a chubby hand as if to try to touch her face, so far out of reach.

"I am Pan. The last of the Mothoc Guardians." To each person's shock, they could understand her as if the words appeared in their minds. "Growing stronger and wiser through the years, for eons I have waited to be with you. And now the Prophecy has come to pass; An'Kru is here to lead us into the Age of Light. But there is much to be accomplished before this can happen."

Pan took a step forward. "An age ago, just after the days of my father, Moc'Tor, a rebel group split from the Mothoc who had followed Straf'Tor to Kayerm. Its members caused great distress, and as a result, their Leader was executed by Straf'Tor himself, and the rest of his followers were expelled from the community. That band has remained alienated, their bitterness growing through the centuries. And because they are Mothoc, their negativity is poisoning the life force that permeates and makes up everything here in your realm of Etera.

"The opening of Kthama Minor and An'Kru's appearance have caused an influx of the life force through the vortex that weaves throughout Etera, circulating the creative power of the One-Who-Is-Three. The rebel Mothoc are connected to the current of the web, just as are any of the Mothoc or Sarnonn. As am I.

"The rebel Mothoc know about the prophecy of An'Kru. They know his coming heralds the Age of Light. Because they have lost their way, in their twisted beliefs, they resent the existence of the

Akassa and Sarnonn. They do not want the Age of Light to dawn; they rather wish to create strife and division on Etera. In time, as An'Kru grows, he will cause the vortex to grow even stronger. And they will realize he has entered this realm. And from that moment on, they will seek him here, hoping to destroy him before he can grow into his full power."

Everyone suddenly looked around, trying to find Adia. Acaraho had left the front of the room to join her, putting his arm around her waist in support.

"Fear not," said Pan. "For now, his presence here is cloaked. But we are racing against time. These Guardians and An'Kru must be taught how to use their abilities. I have already started teaching the six, but An'Kru is yet too young. However, as he grows, and so does his power, even I, on my own, will not be able to conceal his existence here. When that time comes, I will take him with me to keep him safe until he learns to use his powers and can fulfill his destiny."

No, no, no. Adia clutched Acaraho to stop herself from falling.

"So he will remain at Kthama until he reaches the age of seven. At which time he will come with me for his own protection."

"What? No? Go *where*?" Adia stammered.

"For now, he will be loved, cherished, and raised in the care of his parents and community. He will learn the ways of the People. As for the Sarnonn Guardians, I will continue to teach them elsewhere, as I have already been doing, because my presence here pulls too much power from the vortex and could alert the rebels that I have returned. The six female Guardians are seeded. The females will not be given to this battle as their role is one of creation. But their offspring—and in time, the others to come—will take part in the war to save Etera from the negativity of the rebel Mothoc and the Hue'Mahns."

"But heed my words. The battle for Etera does not fall to these of us alone. The future of Etera is in your hands, too—Brothers, Akassa, Sarnonn, Waschini. All who carry Hue'Mahn blood must live in harmony with creation. If An'Kru succeeds in his destiny, a new age will open for Etera, another chance. But if the negative thinking of the Waschini is not corrected, it will take root and spread further.

"Etera wishes to live. She knows the Hue'Mahns present a threat to her. And if we fail, she can, and will, call on those who serve her to rid herself of this population rather than let all the other creatures perish. Let us pray it does not come to that."

The room was utterly silent as Pan moved toward the back and gently handed An'Kru to his mother. Adia wrapped herself around her son and buried them both in Acaraho's arms.

"I leave you now, but not without a little more hope," said Pan. She suddenly vanished and reappeared. Behind her stood thirty or forty Sarnonn, quite a few holding offspring in their arms.

Everyone gasped.

"This is Adik'Tar Notar and his community."

Oh'Dar and his grandparents turned to each other, their eyes wide.

"I ask you to receive them into Kht'shWea."

Haan found his voice, "Of course, Guardian. We welcome them all!"

Pan then moved over to Khon'Tor and stood directly in front of him. "Son of my father's sons, blood of my blood. Return now to your daughter, and to your gentle Tehya and the son who is even now growing peacefully within her belly. Unbind and release the regrets that still hobble your soul, lest they cause you to stumble on the way to your destiny."

She turned and reached her hand out to Nootau, who with Iella had taken a place beside his mother.

He glanced at his mate before slowly approaching Pan. He stood in front of the Mothoc Guardian, looking up at her immense height, waiting.

"You come from greatness. And you have greatness within you," Pan said. "Continue your studies with Urilla Wuti. Learn all you can. And to answer the question troubling your soul, Nootau; no, Acaraho will live for many years yet. And regardless, your path lies in another direction than to become Leader of the High Rocks."

Then she turned to the Brothers. "And you, one of the Great Spirit's greatest gifts to Etera. It is you, those whom my own kind betrayed at the deepest level, in whom lie the hope for the future. Without you, the Sarnonn and the Akassa would not exist. And without the Sarnonn and Akassa, your own future would be brief. But working together, we have a chance of turning the dark tide which, if not stopped, will carry you all to a catastrophic end."

Pan paused a moment and added, "How ironic, you who are the teachers the Hue'Mahns most desperately need to save their own kind, are those to whom they are least willing to listen."

"Hear me now, Healers. I leave you all a gift. Your sensitivities will be further augmented.

For others here, whose abilities have lain dormant, those who perhaps have never thought of themselves as called to be Healers, you will experience a quickening in your soul as your gifts awaken. Until I return, seek the will of the Great Spirit. Trust that you are guided. Love one another."

Pan looked around the room one more time. She raised her hand to Haan and the Sarnonn Guardians and said, "I leave you now—for the time being—to the future of your own making."

Having said all she had come to say, Pan raised both hands into the air and glimmered from sight in front of their eyes.

As the Mothoc Guardian disappeared, Adia felt a surge of energy fill her entire being.

The room broke into chatter, heads turning, some rushing to find comfort in the embrace of a loved one or friend. The crowd parted easily as Haan and his Guardians made their way through to greet Notar and his community. Urilla Wuti joined Adia, Nadiwani, and Acaraho. The Brothers' Chiefs spoke among themselves.

Miss Vivian turned to Oh'Dar, 'What just happened? Did that creature just disappear into thin air?" Her lips were trembling.

"The Mothoc, as well as the Sarnonn, can cloak themselves. I imagine that's what she just did."

"She?" asked Ben.

"Yes," said Oh'Dar. "Later, I'll explain about the Guardian, Pan, and the Mothoc—after things settle down."

"We're living in a fantasy come to life," said Ben.

Iella threw her arms around Nootau. "I did not know you were worried about someday having to lead the People of the High Rocks."

"It is not exactly about leading them. My fear has been about losing Acaraho. That my leading this community would be brought on by something happening to him."

Nootau turned to Adia, still sheltered in Acaraho's arms. "Mama, you do not think for a moment that Pan would let any harm come to An'Kru?"

Adia wiped her tears and stared at her son. "How am I to give him up? How am I to place him in another's care? Was it not enough I had to give you up, and in the time you were out of my arms, you were almost murdered?"

She turned her head back and rested her face against Acaraho's muscular chest. *I am being challenged to surrender what I hold dear. My jealousy at Nootau's turning to Urilla Wuti, his giving her that crystal. My resentment of Haan, feeling that he was withholding information. My fears for An'Kru.*

Acaraho closed his eyes as he held his mate—as if struggling to maintain his own composure.

"When the time comes, I will go with him," said Nootau.

"No!" Iella exclaimed, clasping his hand. "How can you say that? You do not even know where Pan will take him. And for how long."

"I was told that when the time came, I would know without a doubt what my role with An'Kru would be," said Nootau. "And now I know. But I also know that this journey we must take with Pan will not cause us to be separated forever and that he and I will return safely to all of you, whom we love so much."

Iella looked up at him. "Seven years. We have only seven years before you leave?"

Adia pulled back a little from Acaraho's embrace and said to Nootau, "That is why Pan told you to study all you could with Urilla Wuti. To prepare you for whatever awaits you. She knew you were to go with An'Kru."

She looked up at her mate; she could feel his

strength, and the love for her that radiated out of him. She felt Nadiwani standing resolutely at her side. She could feel Urilla Wuti's strength shoring her up and surrounding her with love. She saw Nimida and Tar standing off to the side and could feel their compassion and support. *The family I thought I would never have. I must learn to trust their love for me and allow myself to lean on them. After my father died and I was sent here to Kthama, there was a time when I felt alone. Now I am blessed to be surrounded by so many who care for me and who I care for in return. I am not alone. And neither is An'Kru.*

And through all that has happened to me, I think the biggest thing I have learned is that hard times cannot be prevented; all we can do is to trust that somehow we will find the strength within ourselves to get through them.

⚘

Suddenly, her fears calmed, Adia thought of Khon'Tor and searched the room to see him standing alone. She released herself from Acaraho's embrace, handed An'Kru to Nadiwani, and went over to the High Rocks' fallen Leader.

"You are to have a son," she said gently.

"Another son," Khon'Tor said, looking down at Adia.

"Nootau told me he spoke with you. I do not know if he has spoken with Acaraho; he may have been waiting until this event was behind us. But I agree with Pan," she said. "Find forgiveness for yourself; you have to release your self-hatred. You must not let the past rob you of your future. Or the present.

"Look at him," she said, twisting back to look at Nootau. "He is a blessing to everyone he meets; he is kind of spirit and gentle of soul. And I see the same sweetness in Arismae. And Nimida, who has become a very skilled toolmaker and a sweet, kind-hearted friend to everyone."

She once again looked at Khon'Tor, "It is time to release the specter of Akar'Tor that hangs over you. Whatever happened to make him the tortured soul he was does not exist in any of your other offspring."

"You are wise," Khon'Tor said to her. "Your offspring are blessed by your presence, as are all the People. They always have been."

Adia searched Khon'Tor's eyes and found the pain behind them.

She then did what she had voluntarily done but once before. She reached out and gently placed her hand over Khon'Tor's heart.

She looked deep into his eyes and whispered, "Peace," she said. "Peace. Peace now and forevermore."

Khon'Tor felt a flood of love radiate from the Healer's touch and spread through him. It was like a breeze warmed by passing over an evening fire, and it permeated his every cell. In the Healer's eyes, where there was every right to be resentment and bitterness, he saw only compassion and forgiveness.

He fought back the sting of tears, and placing his hand over hers where it rested on his chest, he closed his eyes. It was the first time he had touched Adia since the night he struck her down and so grievously wronged her. And somehow, that gentle gesture shared between them released both completely from the pain of the past.

Nootau was watching from across the room. He turned to see Acaraho studying him. And Acaraho said, "You know, do you not? Somehow you know."

"Yes. But it does not change anything between you and me," Nootau said.

Acaraho put his arms around the young male he had raised as his own. He hugged him tightly, and choking back so many emotions, whispered, "You are my son. *My son.*"

Nootau tightened his grasp on the only father he had ever known and whispered back. "Yes, Father. I am and always will be your son. No power on Etera or anywhere in creation can ever change that."

E'ranale, Apenimon 'Mok, An'Kru, and Pan stood together watching from the Corridor.

"Even from the peace and safety of here, we live every moment with them, do we not?" said Pan.

Apenimon watched his daughter heal the one who had at one point sought to destroy her. "Love is a bond that nothing can break. No distance, no circumstance, no power, can rend it. There is no darkness, no storm that can put out its light. It is that which inspires us, encourages us, heals us, binds us one to another in innumerable ways of the heart and soul. And every step in between, no matter how difficult, is ordered and protected. Love is the song from which the One-Who-Is-Three sings us into being. It is love that calls us home to itself. It is love from which we spring and love to which we return. In the end, it is always love that saves us."

He stopped a moment before saying, "My daughter's journey is long still, with many trials and troubles to come. But if she can focus on hearing love's voice, it will guide her, and everyone she loves, through the storms and safely back home."

PLEASE READ
A FINAL NOTE ABOUT SERIES ONE

When I first published this book, I did it stating that there would be a pause between the end of this book and the next. Well, that pause has come to a close. The next book in the series, is Book Twelve: The Blade of Truth.

Now, if you have not read any of Series Two: Wrak-Wavara: The Age of Darkness I surely hope you will. Readers who have read The Age of Darkness have said it is as interesting as the first and recommend that everyone read it. Series Two takes us back in time to the story of the Mothoc, the Ancient Sasquatch, as they wrestle with difficult choices in their effort to avoid extinction. Book One will encompass a small portion of the material presented during Series One in Book Six: Revelation. However, there's a great deal of detail woven around and in addition to the material already presented. At the moment, there are five books in Series Two. I do not believe that there will be more, but I am apt to change my mind as you can see!

Email me at leigh@leighrobertsauthor.com

Thank you for all the kind words of encouragement and appreciation that so many of you have expressed throughout this first series. I hope you'll continue with me on this journey and that the next series will entertain you as well as this one seems to have.

Blessings – Leigh Roberts

Book One: Khon'Tor's Wrath
Book Two: The Healer's Mantle
Book Three: Oh'Dar's Quest
Book Four: The Healer's Blade
Book Five: Contact
Book Six: Revelation
Book Seven: The Edge of The Age
Book Eight: The Wall of Records
Book Nine: Retribution
Book Ten: Endings and Beginnings
Book Eleven: The Edge of Hope
Book Twelve: The Blade of Truth

Books in Series Two:
Book One: The Age of Darkness
Book Two: The Chamber of the Ancients
Book Three: The Secret of the Leader's Staff
Book Four: The End of the Age
Book Five: Out of the Dust of Etera

AN INTERVIEW WITH THE CHARACTERS, WHO WERE WAITING TOGETHER TO SPEAK WITH ME.

Acaraho: This is a better place to leave us than the way things were at the end of Book Ten. I am grateful for that. But what do we do now? Hang around for seven years until Pan returns for An'Kru? That seems a lot to ask. And frankly, I am worried about Adia.

LR: I suspect you'll find your turn comes around more quickly than you think.

Acaraho: That is good. I do get befuddled by the time continuum in fiction. But what about my mate?

Adia: I have faith that it will work out. I have seven years to spend with An'Kru. And Acaraho, there is much you need to teach him while he is with us. All the things you taught Oh'Dar and Nootau. And Nootau and Iella have seven years to solidify their love and perhaps have offspring of their own! I am not making light, though; to let An'Kru and Nootau leave with Pan will be one of the hardest things I have ever had to do.

LR: I'm glad you're working this out, but I'm not sure there will be a whole seven years between where this leaves off and when it starts up again.

Adia: Even better. Thank you for the ray of hope.

Tehya: I must say that I am thrilled to be seeded again and to know I will give Khon'Tor a son!

Khon'Tor: I am also happy to hear it. It seems that when one door closes, another door opens.

LR: That's life, isn't it? It's filled with challenges and victories. There are times to climb mountains and times to rest and replenish in the sweet meadows. You all have so many more experiences ahead of you. But I promise never to give you more than you can bear.

Oh'Dar: I'm happy that Pajackok and I seem to be repairing our relationship; I've missed having him as a friend. And he and Snana do seem like a great match.

Acise: I cannot wait to meet our offspring. Will it be a boy or a girl? Will he or she have Oh'Dar's blue eyes? There is much for us to look forward to.

Oh'Dar: I have to admit though, Leigh, I'm worried about Snide Tucker. He's up to something.

LR: I wish I could say you're wrong, but—

Oh'Dar: I knew it!

LR: Ben and Miss Vivian, would you like to say anything?

Miss Vivian: I've no regrets about coming. I can't imagine having missed this. I also appreciate everything Grayson has done to make us comfortable, though I do miss butter.

Ben: I second that. I feel like I'm twenty again with my whole life ahead of me. And I miss butter too. And bread.

LR: I'd also miss them. I'm not sure I could give

up bread or butter. I'll put that on your wish list. Anything else?

Ben: Eggs. Milk. A little spiced cider now and then to take the edge off.

Miss Vivian: The summer breeze coming through a window at night.

LR: That one is a little more difficult, but there isn't any reason you couldn't sleep outside in the summer. There are watchers everywhere; you'd be safe! Khon'Tor has done it many times.

Miss Vivian: What a lovely idea, thank you!

LR: Anyone else? *I looked around the room, giving them a chance to think.*

Haan: Having Notar's people brought to us is a blessing for both our communities. And wherever they were living cannot possibly compare to life at Kht'shWea.

LR: I'm sure that's true. But home is home, and it will still be an adjustment for them. It's nice to see so many little ones who will soon be running through your halls.

Haaka: I am worried about Kalli. She is the only one of her kind. Who will love her? Will she live a life of loneliness and isolation?

Adia got up to sit next to Haaka.

Adia: I so understand your pain. No parent wants their offspring to face hardship. We must trust that Leigh will find a way to free her from a life of unhappiness.

LR: Oh gee. No pressure there, thank goodness. Now, on a final note, I'm excited about what the future holds for all of us. Blessings to you and to our readers; I'm grateful for their loyalty and continued interest in this journey we're all taking together.

ACKNOWLEDGMENTS

Many of you have commented on the spiritual ideas woven through these stories. Those of you interested in the evolution of human consciousness no doubt recognize some of the universal truths I've laced into these books, some of which are just starting to emerge in larger numbers of our population as more and more of us seek spiritual awakening.

For example, in this book I bring into the dialogue between E'ranale and Adia the idea of distorted or dark pleasure. This concept isn't new to our consciousness. The Germans even have a term for it, "Schadenfreude."

Merriam-Webster defines Schadenfreude as "Enjoyment obtained from the troubles of others."

In Book Ten, I mentioned the Uni-Verse, the One Song. I don't know the origin of this phrase, as I haven't been able to trace the original attribution. To me, this is just another example of the spiritual ideas that surface through a variety of channels as we become ready to accept them.

🐾

On a personal note, there are very few pets mentioned in The Etera Chronicles. The only two are Kweeuu, Oh'Dar's wolf, and Waki, the wolf cub gifted to Oh'Dar by Khon'Tor after Tehya had taken over the affections of Kweeuu.

But for many of us, our pets are one of our greatest blessings. Many of you have shared pictures of your pets on the The Etera Chronicles private Facebook group. Our love for our pets is one of the common threads that bind us together. I, for one, would no longer want to live in a world where I couldn't have a pet.

So to represent all the furbabies we have loved and lost, and those who walk among us still, here are some pictures of Hope.

Hope was rescued as a tiny orphaned kitten, only a few days old. Kathi, her adopted mom, nursed her to health against the veterinarian's warning that there was little hope the kitten would survive. Hope enjoyed the next seventeen years of her life surrounded by the love of the woman who saved her, until Hope passed in 2020.

So for all of us who love or have loved a beloved pet, our hope is that we will see them again, along with our other beloveds, in the Corridor where there will nevermore be tears, or sorrow, or the heartbreak of separation.

So in a way, we're all living on The Edge of Hope.

✿

Lastly, I would be sorely remiss in not thanking my husband, family, friends, and readers for their continued support. And an additional huge heartfelt thank you to my fantastic editor, who has stayed the journey with me, and who promises to put up with me through the next two series. Thank you, Joy, you are irreplaceable.

Made in the USA
Las Vegas, NV
09 February 2024